## Change of plans

Kellon kept an eye on the boat as it bobbed up and down in the breaking surf. The pilot was revving the engine now and then, trying to keep the boat in the same general spot. The third man was standing as best as he could in the rocking boat, holding on with one hand while clutching a semi-automatic rifle with the other.

Shortman handed his backpack to Blackie then turned to pick up the money. As he took a step back towards Kellon with the payment, he heard a command from Blackie and froze.

"Wait! Don't move!" came the husky voice of the Vincentian.
Kellon could not believe his eyes and ears. He pulled out his Glock and held it against his right leg.
"Blackie, what you doing?"
"Shut up! Change of plans."

Blackie was now pointing a pistol at Shortman. "Bring back the money!"

# WHITE SPICE

D. E. AMBROSE

ISBN-13: 978-1514355886
ISBN-10: 1514355884

Cover design by Jean Renel Pierre Louis (Prensnelo)
Email: jeanrenelp@yahoo.fr

Author's photo by David Sayers

Map of Grenada retrieved from http://www.d-maps.com/carte.php?num_car=66485&lang=en
and modified by D.E. Ambrose

Email: whitespice2015@gmail.com

# DEDICATION

To all my former English teachers and professors
and
the hardworking men and women of the Royal Grenada Police Force.

ACKNOWLEDGEMENTS

O Lord my God, I will give thanks unto thee for ever. (Psalm 30: 12)

To my family and friends for encouraging me to plough ahead with this project.

To the following departments and members of the Royal Grenada Police Force (RGPF): the Community Relations Department; Inspector Simon Dickson of the Drug Squad; Sergeant Bobby Medford of the Grenada Coast Guard; Assistant Superintendent Solomon Stafford; Assistant Superintendent A. Kirabi Belfon; Inspector M. Simon Douglas and the 2015 Police Studies class of the T.A. Marryshow Community College.

To Suelin Low Chew Tung for her invaluable assistance.

To Jean Renel Pierre Louis (Prensnelo) for his amazing artwork for the cover.

To David Sayers for the author's photoshoot.

To Dorothy Tsakani Haukozi for her loving support.

# THE ISLAND OF GRENADA

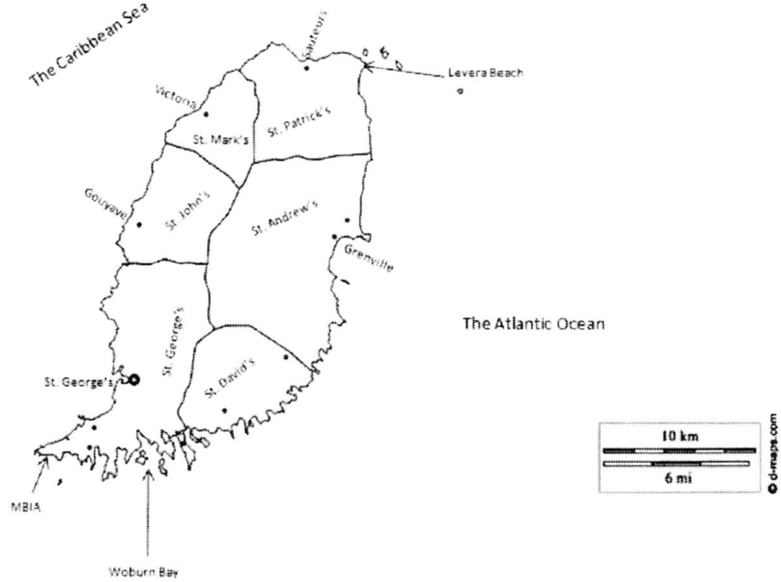

# WHITE SPICE

# PROLOGUE

Tuesday December 11, 2012
St. George's, Grenada

**4:45 p.m.**

Luis was relieved to be back on board his ship and headed straight for his cabin. He couldn't believe that once again the cops hadn't searched him before allowing him to pass onto the pier. The senior officer at the checkpoint simply glanced at ID cards and waved the visitors on, as the line to pass through the X ray machine was getting long. Security seems very lax in this country, he thought, somewhat alarmed. He stored the backpack in his locker, making sure the padlock was engaged. In four days he would hand the bag over to someone in Puerto Rico. He collapsed on his bunk and slipped into Dreamland.

**Three hours earlier**

Luis looked at his watch for about the one hundredth time. He wasn't nervous, just eager to do this errand and return to the ship. This was his fourth trip to Grenada since he joined the kitchen crew of the mega cruise ship. The ship visited the Spice Isle every Tuesday morning at eight and stayed in port for twelve hours, allowing its three thousand five hundred passengers to explore the one hundred and twenty square-mile island. The crew took three hours of shore leave, in shifts. He would get his chance to walk on dry land at two p.m. He mentally reviewed the errand for the umpteenth time since the ship berthed on the Cruise Ship Terminal in the island's capital, St. George's. He had done this task three times before and knew the process like the back of his hand, but he didn't want to make any mistakes. There was no way he was going to cross El Caballo back in Miami. That man was crazy, and nobody in his right mind would double-cross Miami's second biggest drug kingpin. It was rumoured that El Caballo had once personally slung one of his lieutenants naked over a bridge one night. The man was El Caballo's own cousin who had been photographed sharing a passionate kiss with one of the drug lord's many women. Luis certainly wasn't going to botch this exchange.

Luis was instructed to take a bus to the northern town of Sauteurs to collect something from someone called Boss. He would be emailed the license plate number of a specific bus that would take him to a place called Leapers Hill. He had made the exchange each of the last three weeks, and every time someone different met him when he got off the bus. He thought it was interesting that, so far, only young girls arrived to escort him to a big orange house that dominated a hill above the historic town. He was never sure if he had actually met this Boss, as no one introduced himself by that name. Someone would take his bag and disappear into one of the many rooms only to return with it precisely five minutes later. He knew he was dropping off money and suspected that he was collecting drugs of some kind. He dared not open any of the packages, but the load on the return trip to St. George's would always be much heavier. He always took the trip down the Western Main Road with the same bus that brought him up. This delivery and pickup system seemed well-organised.

At five minutes past two, Luis' Blackberry pinged, signalling an incoming message. He quickly accessed his Hotmail and memorized the plate number of the bus for today's trip. Then he deleted the message. He put on a purple Grenada souvenir t-shirt and tucked it into his khaki shorts. Then he put on a pair of white calf-length sports socks and slipped into some tennis shoes. He grabbed his Rayban sunglasses, picked up his green backpack and headed for the gangway. He shook his head as he thought about the precise instructions given to him for his attire for each trip. Apparently, someone didn't think being the only Hispanic male walking among the natives in a rural town was enough to be easily identified. He smiled at himself as he passed in front of a mirror, flashing two gold incisors embedded in the upper jaw. He pulled out a Canon digital camera and slung it around his neck to complete his cover as a clueless visitor to the island.

Inspector Ricky Andrews stood on the pier of the cruise ship terminal and looked up at the ship towering over him. He marvelled at the immense size of this floating hotel. Maybe one day he would be able to take a Caribbean cruise. He lowered his gaze to see his partner, Corporal Nichelle Peters, walking towards him as if she were a visiting passenger from the ship. In fact, they were both pretending to be tourists, part of their cover to try to detect any illegal activities that the precious guests may be engaged in. They were part of a team of specially-trained officers of the Royal Grenada Police Force that comprised the elite Drug Squad One (DS-1) of the Drug Interdiction Agency. Officers of DS-1 were deployed across the country as part of the effort to fight cocaine trafficking.

Ever since the United States Department of State had labelled Grenada as a major drug transhipment location, the American government had spent millions of dollars to fund training and provide equipment for the DIA, which was made up of three drug squads. Every member of DS-1 was trained in the United States, and some had seen action in the field, in South America and Mexico. Most spoke Spanish, and Inspector Andrews was a fluent speaker of the language. He was, in fact, the deputy head of the DIA, and he always led from the front. With a Bachelor's degree in Foreign Languages, Andrews spoke Spanish, French and German fluently, and could also communicate effectively in Italian and Chinese Mandarin. At five feet ten inches, Andrews easily fit in anywhere. Today, he was playing the role of tourist perfectly, taking photos of the city and the ship. The taller Corporal Peters, stopped at his side, smiling.

"He comin'," she said excitedly.

"OK, les' take some pictures," Andrews suggested. "Make sure you get him in dem."

Andrews posed with the ship in the background, flexing his biceps and making Peters laugh. Anyone passing would think they were a newly married couple. Peters aimed her camera at him and zoomed in, snapping a few shots as he changed his poses. With each click she got a better shot of the six-foot tall muscular Hispanic man in the purple t-shirt as he got closer. Anyone inspecting her pictures would note that half of Andrews' body was not even in the shot as she tried to get good exposures of the figure in the purple t-shirt who had no idea that he was being photographed. Not bad-looking at all, she thought. But who was he? DS-1 knew only that for three consecutive weeks he would take a bus alone to Sauteurs, and meet with a different girl each time. How did he know these girls? Facebook? Tagged? Instagram? Was there a prostitution ring up there? What was in the backpack? They needed to know who this man was and what his activities were when he travelled to Sauteurs. She walked up to the inspector and they started to review the pictures.

Suddenly, Andrews had a brainwave. He wiped the camera with his shirt then called out to a receding Luis.

"Sir, kyan you take a pic of me and my fiancée?" he shouted in his best Jamaican accent.

"Sure, Dude," Luis agreed, smiling broadly.

He came over, took the camera from Andrews and pointed it at the two officers as they embraced passionately, as any loving couple on a tropical vacation would.

"Say cheese," he said, pressing the shutter button. His Latino inflection was easily detectable.

"Tanx a lot, mon," Peters said, smiling toothily at him.

Andrews also thanked Luis in his best Jamaican-accented Spanish, put out his right hand, palm flat, so that the visitor could rest the digital device on it. The muscular Hispanic thought nothing of this strange way in which the undercover officer received the camera, but nodded and continued on to the Welcome Centre and Esplanade

Mall. Andrews turned around so that his back was to the retreating Luis and put the camera in a plastic bag. He placed it in Peters' rather large handbag. She looked at him enquiringly.

"Fingerprints," he explained.

"Oh. Man, you is ah genius!"

Luis easily found the red Toyota Hiace minibus selected for today's trip and took a seat all the way in the back. It was actually a minivan capable of holding eighteen passengers. He knew from experience that the bus operator and conductor (the person who mans the door for the passengers and collects money) would usually fit twenty-five people in this wide-bodied vehicle. The few windows were very small, which made the interior very hot unless they were moving at a brisk pace. The a/c was seldom used. The stereo system was belting out a fast melodious beat, and the heavy baseline made Luis' internal organs vibrate. Although the lyrics came crystal clear to Luis, he just couldn't put them together in a sentence to understand what the song was about. However, he was impressed that almost all the passengers would sing the chorus together. At least he got the part that "Santa looking for a wife". He overheard one dancing girl telling another that this song was a "bad bad soca-parang".

The northbound trip up the west coast was as hair-raising as always. Luis couldn't understand why the passengers seemed so calm while the vehicle appeared to fly along the narrow roads. At times, vehicles travelling south passed only inches from them. Although the wind was now blowing freely in the bus, Luis was sweating profusely. This ride was scaring the daylights out of him! He was glad his shades were mirrored so that nobody could see the fear in his eyes. The conductor grinned at him for a moment. *Cabrón*, Luis hissed under his breath.

The bus arrived in Sauteurs in a record forty minutes and dropped Luis off at Leapers Hill. He was relieved that he was walking on solid ground again. He had read somewhere that these trips usually took about sixty-five minutes. This driver is *loco*. Twice he had almost thrown up when the bus hurtled around corners. And the offensive body odours of the sweaty schoolgirls that diffused throughout the under-ventilated vehicle had further increased his discomfort. He put his backpack on his back and looked around. As he walked towards a vendor to buy a bottle of water, a slim young lady approached him. She was wearing a short jeans skirt and sandals, while a red spaghetti-strapped top hung loosely over her almost flat chest.

"See-ñor Luis!" she called out.

"Yes."

"Come with me!"

"Lemme get some water."

Luis bought a half-litre bottle of spring water and walked two steps behind the girl up the street. She looked to be about twenty-one, with hard calves. He eyed her backside as she strode on, feeling a tingle in his groin. Damn, how much he missed his wife in Miami, and mistress in San Juan, Puerto Rico. But he wasn't going to mess around with the natives in this country.

They arrived at the house on the hill in five minutes. Luis was huffing and puffing like a locomotive. The girl hadn't even broken a sweat. She sat calmly on the veranda wall, legs slightly open just enough to allow anyone to see her yellow underwear. A shirtless youth emerged from what seemed like a kitchen and stretched out his hand to take Luis' backpack.

"See-dung dey!" he directed Luis, pointing to a plastic chair.

Luis was impressed with himself that he understood what the youth said. He nodded and sat on the chair to admire the view of the rocks offshore to the north. Somewhere out there, Grenada's submarine volcano lies quietly for the time being. This would not be a good time for Kick 'em Jenny to erupt, he mused.

"What's your name?" he asked the girl.

"Crystelle."

She smiled slightly, opening her legs a bit wider.

"Do you go to school?"

"I finish school so long," she declared indignantly. "I is ah big woman, yuh know!"

She opened her legs even more and Luis sighed. What was he doing in this place? Why was he risking his life and his family for this? He recalled the night he was approached by El Caballo's people at the Dolphin Mall in Miami. They had offered him $4000 to do each drop and pickup in three islands. They had also threatened to kill his daughters if he refused. He'd reluctantly agreed, justifying his actions by thinking he was saving his family. These guys had people everywhere. He suspected one of his neighbours to be a spy for El Caballo. How else could she afford such an expensive house and a 2012 Lexus sedan and be unemployed? He knew he was taking a huge risk. He shuddered when he thought about prison in a third world country. But he took comfort in thinking that the law enforcement officials in Grenada didn't seem too vigilant, and were too eager to please the tourist. After all, they needed American dollars. Crystelle interrupted his thoughts.

"I live just up de road. You want to come by me?"

"That's OK, I have to get back," he replied almost scornfully.

She shrugged disappointedly and leaned back some more on her perch, prompting Luis to get up to take a closer look at the rocks and islets offshore. He was relieved when the shirtless youth returned with his backpack. Five minutes. Amazing! The boy could hardly keep it from dragging on the floor. He passed it to Luis. The strong American easily slung the bag over his shoulders and onto his back then immediately took off in the direction of the Sauteurs bus stand for his return trip to St. George's. He wanted to get out of this town quickly, but he wasn't really looking forward to the drive down to the capital. He stepped slowly up to the same bus that had brought him to this rural town, surprised that he was the first person to board. This time he sat up front beside the driver, placing his backpack on the empty seat between the two of them. The bus took off after two more persons stepped in. He couldn't see one of the passengers sending a text on his smartphone nor could he know that the text was directed to Inspector Andrews of DS-1.

About seventy-five minutes later, Luis was buying spices from the vendors in the plaza outside the Esplanade Mall in St. George's. There seemed to be hundreds of young people just milling around. Among them was a twenty-two-year old operative of DS-1 who was sitting on a bench listening to music on an Ipod. The agent, Derek Michaels, looked around lazily, pointing his cell phone in the direction of Luis as the latter was browsing through some souvenirs with a vendor. The video app was active. Luis entered the mall, disappearing through the automatic glass doors. Michaels texted another DS-1 agent on the pier end of the complex to expect Luis then headed to KFC to get some chicken and fries.

# 2013

# CHAPTER 1

**Monday January 14**
**St. Patrick's Secondary School**
**Sauteurs, St. Patrick's**

Jeffrey Alexander and Andy Rupert headed to their spot below the mahogany tree behind the gym to eat their lunch. The two Fifth-Formers always spent the forty-minute lunch break eating and talking about classes, sports and/or girls. Jeffrey often wanted to talk about sports, as he aspired to become a professional footballer in the English Premier League. Andy always wondered why he never put as much effort into his classes as he did into football. At sixteen and five feet ten inches, Jeffrey was already a midfielder on the Grenada national senior team. This made him very popular with the girls of the St. Patrick's Secondary School, and indeed the entire parish of St. Patrick's.

"I kyant wait for the match this weekend," Jeffrey began, opening his bowl of oil-down. "The Gunners will mash up Liverpool."

"Boy, Arsenal lose that game already," countered Andy. The six foot two-inch slender youth played centre back on the school's football team.

"Yeah right!"

Andy sniffed the air, catching the scent of the slightly salty breadfruit, dumplings, pig tail, chicken back, and veggies that made up Jeffrey's oil-down.

"Boy, you brother does cook ah wicked oil-down," he remarked. "That thing smell real good!"

"You telling me!"

Jeffrey offered his pal two dumplings, a piece of breadfruit, a piece of chicken and a portion of pig tail. Both boys ate in silence, savouring the favourite dish of most Grenadians.

"Yow, you want to see something?" Jeffrey suddenly asked excitedly.

Andy opened both hands in front of him, palms up, questioningly.

Jeffrey pulled out a small transparent plastic bag that contained about three tablespoons of a white powder and showed it to his best friend. Andy looked at it, unimpressed.

"So, why you showing me some white sugar?"

"Boy, that's not white sugar," Jeffrey retorted. He looked around furtively and lowered his voice. "Da is cocaine."

Andy recoiled as if Jeffrey had spat at him.

"Boy, you crazy? You want to put us in trouble? Put that away!"

Jeffrey laughed. He explained how he "pinched" a bit from his cousin's stash, but Andy wasn't even listening to him.

"Jeff, man, I not hanging with you while you have this thing. I have exams and kyant afford to geh kick out ah school. You know is zero tolerance for drugs on the compound!"

Undoubtedly, Andy was very nervous, and he was looking around to see if anyone was checking them out under the tree. To his horror, he saw a thin female figure approaching. It was Petisha, a Form Four student who had a huge crush on Jeffrey. As usual, her yellow shirt was not tucked into her green school skirt as it should be. Her tie was too long, the tip reaching about ten inches below her white belt. Her hair was dishevelled as if she had just woken up. She was obviously heading straight for the two boys.

"Jeff, put that away," Andy barked. "Petisha coming."

"Don't worry, man. She won't tell nobody," Jeffrey reassured Andy. He put the plastic bag in his backpack anyway.

Petisha came up and surveyed the two friends. At eighteen, she was older than most students in Form Four. She was the second of nine siblings, all living with their mother. She never knew who her father was. She often came to school for only three days per week because her mother couldn't afford to send her every day. She really liked Jeffrey and took every opportunity to interact with him. *If only I wasn't so poor*, she would say to herself. She lived in a two-bedroom plywood house with her mother and siblings. They didn't even have electricity in the house. Their toilet and bathroom were structures built outside the house and made from sheets of rusty galvanized zinc. Jeffrey, on the other hand, lived in a massive orange house on High Street that had an awesome view of the rocks and islands of the southern Grenadines to the north, and of the rest of the town of Sauteurs to the south-west. They were from totally different socioeconomic worlds. She had made up her mind to do whatever it took to be with Jeffrey, even if they hooked up for only a few days or weeks.

She greeted the famous young footballer cheerily. "Hi, Jeffy!"

Jeffrey winced inwardly as she greeted him by that moniker. He could never understand why she couldn't figure out that he didn't like her. She dressed poorly, she spoke badly, and she hardly wore deodorant. Most times he smelled her before he even saw her.

"Yes, Petisha," he replied.

"Wha' you ha for lunch today?"

"I done eat already."

Andy interrupted, "Hey, Jeff, I gone. I leaving you two lovebirds alone."

Jeffrey looked at Andy with an expression that pleaded for him to stay. However, Andy turned on his heels and headed back to his classroom.

Jeffrey turned back to find Petisha grinning at him.

"So wat's up, Jeffy?"

"Look, Petisha, I don't like when you call me so."

"How you mean? Dat's a nice pet name for you."

Jeffrey shook his head like a defeated man and sighed. *Change the subject*, he thought. He pulled out the plastic bag with the powder.

"Gyul, you want some nose candy?"

"Wah is dat? I eatin' anything right now, fus I hungry. I might eat you and all!"

"You mean you don't know what nose candy is?" Jeffery asked incredulously. "Try some," he added jokingly.

"But how it little bit so? Dat kyan' full my belly!"

Jeffrey was amazed that Petisha didn't know that nose candy was cocaine. Didn't she see movies where they use this stuff? Lucky for him, he was around his cousin and older brother to see them deal with the drug and to learn some jargon from them. While he was lost in his own thoughts for a few seconds, Petisha grabbed the plastic bag.

"Lemme see how it smell first," she said excitedly, as if she were about to sample chocolate at a confectionary.

"Wait!" Jeffrey shouted, but he was too late to stop her from burying her nose in the bag.

In one huge snort, Petisha inhaled close to a teaspoon of the drug. The effects were almost immediate. Her heart rate increased dramatically and she was almost certain Jeffrey was hearing the pounding inside her chest. Jeffrey noticed that she was sweating as hard as a labourer in the midday sun, and breathing very heavily too. He himself started to sweat in fear. This wasn't supposed to happen. Nobody was supposed to sample the stuff. If his cousin finds out, he is dead!

Petisha looked at Jeffrey with a puzzled expression.

"Wah you gi' me dey?" she gasped.

"I didn't mean for you to do that," he replied, his voice quivering. "That's cocaine."

"What!"

Petisha's knees buckled and she sat on the ground, leaning against the tree to steady herself, as she was suddenly feeling dizzy.

"Jeffy!" she cried out in alarm.

What was happening to her? Her heart was beating even faster.

She was having trouble breathing. Her head was pounding. Her stomach was churning. She felt like vomiting. She began to retch.

Jeffrey felt helpless as he watched Petisha's condition get worse. He had no idea what to do. He didn't mean to hurt her. She looked like she was about to die. He handed her his translucent blue water bottle. He didn't plan to ask for it back as she took a swig then started throwing up. The sight of the vomit was too much for him. He was beginning to feel nauseous also. He had to get out of there. Amazingly, with the presence of mind to pick up the small bag of remaining coke, Jeffrey grabbed his gear and took off. The usually confident athlete was now a scared puppy heading for a hole in the school fence.

Petisha called out feebly after the retreating boy, "Help me, Jeff."

The pain in her chest was getting more intense and was taking up more of her attention than the throbbing headache. With her blood vessels constricted, her heart was being taxed heavily to perform its duty. It was a losing battle for the malnourished girl. She thought about her mother, her three brothers and five sisters. She thought about Jeffrey, and tears rolled down her cheeks. She suddenly grabbed her left breast and fell backwards, at the same time throwing up for the last time. Less than five minutes after Petisha had greeted Jeffrey, she was dead.

Petisha's prone body was discovered by a group of Form One students heading to the playing field for Physical Education twenty-seven minutes later. Their screams alerted teachers and other students. The Principal, Ruth Sampson, rushed to the scene accompanied by a security guard. She looked at the body of the young lady lying beside the tree and her previous training as a registered nurse with eighteen years of experience took over. She pressed her right index and middle fingers against Petisha's neck to check the carotid artery for a pulse, but found none. She took one look at the white powder smeared around the dead girl's nose, and the contents of her stomach caked in a line down the side of her cheeks, and suspected the cause of death. With the help of teachers and the security guard, she herded the hysterical students back to the main compound then used her personal cellphone to call the police and the Ministry of Education. She looked at her watch. It was 12:34 p.m. Mrs. Sampson and the St. Patrick's Secondary School were suddenly pulled into the national conversation on drugs. If that powder was cocaine as she suspected, where did this girl get the drug? She was too poor to buy the stuff, so who gave it to her? Did she die of a heart attack or did she drown in her own vomit? The Principal wasn't looking forward to the rest of the week, dealing with the detectives from the Criminal Investigation Department and the thorough investigation that was sure to follow. Her greatest dread, however, was bringing the grim news to Petisha's mother. She began a slow gait to her office to make the call to the single mother whose brood was suddenly reduced to eight children. She sighed heavily.

At 3:55 p.m., the undertakers took away Petisha's body. However, a crowd remained outside the locked gate at the entrance to the compound. A black 2011 Nissan X-Trail with tinted windows drove by slowly, its two male occupants wondering what the commotion was all about. They were surprised to see the high level of agitation in the crowd. Two uniformed officers of the RGPF stood guard at the closed gate. It was even more puzzling that not even a single head turned to scrutinise the vehicle that crawled by with shiny gold spinning rims, the heavy baseline of a *Daddy Yankee* Reggaeton beat wafting out of the tinted half-opened front windows. The vehicle drove on for a half mile down the road before pulling into a garage connected to a big orange house.

# CHAPTER 2

**Alexander Residence**
**High Street**
**Sauteurs, St. Patrick's**

Junior Alexander walked out of the garage with his cousin, Kellon, after parking his black Nissan X-Trail, and looked back up the road in the direction of the secondary school. They could think of no reason why the police would be at the school at this late hour of the day. Maybe there was a serious fight, and someone got stabbed.

"Boy, what you feel happen up there?" Kellon voiced both their thoughts. The evening sun was glinting off his bald head, and he used a green rag to wipe the moisture from his glistening crown.

"Beats me. We'll find out from Jeff."

They turned toward the house. Junior could never stop admiring the mansion whenever he left or returned home. It was the pride of his family. It was a two-storey brick structure with a floor space of over twenty-five hundred square feet that dominated the town of Sauteurs. The modern Mediterranean look made it somewhat of a tourist attraction in this rural section of Grenada that was considered the poorest part of the country. Visitors would often pose in front of the house to take pictures. The tourists often made sure they got the much smaller neighbouring wooden houses in their shots, which demonstrated the contrast of rich and poor in the rural community.

The massive house was completed in fifteen months, and when, in August of 2003, the Alexander family finally moved in, they were the talk of the town. Everyone speculated about where they got the money to construct this huge and very expensive home. Then one morning in December 2003, Junior's father, John, was spotted on the veranda in a wheelchair. Only his family knew that he was involved in a very serious accident on his construction site in Ft. Lauderdale, Florida, in 1998.

John Alexander was a foreman at the site of a hotel project. An overloaded cement mixer had toppled over, falling on him, crushing his legs, breaking several ribs and his back. It was a miracle that he had survived. He had spent two long years in hospital and underwent over sixteen surgeries. Both the construction company he worked for and the company that provided cement to the site settled with him, compensating him with tens of millions of American dollars. With this large award, the family built the mansion, bought a fishing boat and a pleasure cruiser, opened an electronics and appliances store, and invested a percentage in real estate in Grenada and Barbados. They spread the rest of the money in accounts in several banks in the name of each member of the immediate family. John Alexander died in May 2004 from complications from his injuries.

Junior winced for the millionth time at the orange colour that stained the landscape. He shook his head in slight embarrassment, his short locks flinging from side to side. He hated that colour, but it was his mother's wish and he had to respect it. She never wanted a big house but she always wanted a home painted orange. He remembered the broad smile on her face, the way her eyes lit up as she saw the finished mansion for the first time. He didn't know at the time that she was dying from breast cancer. She succumbed to the disease eight months after moving into their High Street home.

"Jeff!" Junior called out as he and Kellon entered the huge French aluminium front doors into the main hall.

"Yow! I watching a game in here," Jeffrey answered from the living room.

Junior and Kellon entered the spacious living room and were not surprised to find Jeffrey looking at a football match on the 55-inch LED TV.

"Who playing?" Kellon enquired.

"Real Madrid and Barcelona. Is just a rerun of the first *El Clásico* from last year."

Junior got straight to the point. "Wha' happen in school today?"

"What you mean?" Jeffrey seemed genuinely surprised.

"It have plenty people by the school. And police up there too."

"I don't know nah. I come home since before three to watch those games."

"Well, call somebody and find out," Kellon suggested.

*I'm your love doctor, call me, anytime you need me, Baby,* . . . It was Jeffrey's Romain Virgo ring tone. He looked at the display on his Blackberry and recognised Andy's number. He let the song play for a few more seconds then picked up the call.

"Yow."

"Jeff, you ain't hear what happen in school?"

"Nah. Junior just telling me it have plenty people up there now."

"Boy, where you was? Why you didn't come back to class?"

"I had something to do. What happened?"

"Hmm. You and Petisha? Boy, the girl dead. What you do the girl?"

"Wha'!?" Jeffrey's knees buckled and he crashed backwards into the sofa.

Junior and Kellon observed him curiously. Beads of sweat had suddenly formed on his forehead and were rolling down his face. His hands were shaking visibly.

"What happen, Jeff?" Junior asked, very concerned.

Jeffrey's mind was reeling. He was sure he was the last person to see Petisha alive. Did anyone besides Andy see them together below the tree? He thought back to the encounter, trying to remember if he had left anything that would lead back to him.

"Man, what you mean Petisha dead?" Although he was pretending to be shocked, the quiver in his voice was genuine. He felt a bit responsible for her death.

Junior and Kellon exchanged glances. They knew Petisha was a girl who really wanted to be with Jeffrey. But he usually shunned her. Now they were baffled about why he seemed to be taking this news of her death so emotionally.

"Yes, man. They find her dead below the tree. What you do her?"

"What you mean what I do her?" Jeffrey shouted. He then remembered he wasn't alone in the room, and froze. This didn't escape the notice of his brother and cousin.

"Take it easy, Jeff," Andy tried to calm Jeffrey. "I not accusing you of anything. But you was the last person to be with her."

"How you know that? You know when I left there? You don't know if anybody pass there after me." There was obvious irritation and fear in Jeffrey's voice.

"Aright, aright, check you later if I hear anything," Andy said. He hung up.

Jeffrey held the phone to his ear for a few seconds even after Andy had hung up. He couldn't look at his brother after he finally put it down. He sighed as he recalled the distress in which he had left Petisha.

"Jeff!" Kellon's booming voice jolted him back to the present. "Well, tell us what happen, nuh."

"Andy that say that Petisha dead in school."

"You mean your girl Petisha?" Junior asked, somewhat teasingly.

"She not my girl. And yes."

"What happen to her? And if she is not your girl, why you acting like that?" Junior watched him closely.

"What you talking about? I will get upset if anybody from school dead," Jeff responded, a bit too evasively.

"Fair enough," Junior said. "But you saw her today? It sound like Andy think you and she did something together."

"Not really. She was just hounding me for lunch."

"Really?" Kellon chimed in sarcastically. "You sure you didn't bring the girl behind the gym for something?" He laughed, slapping palms with Junior in a five.

"Man, this is serious thing. I didn't do anything with the girl. I left her after I saw her."

"OK, OK, I hear you." Kellon put his arm around Jeffrey's shoulder.

"Man, just find out what really went on up there," Junior said. "I don't like when police so close to us. We going in the den for a while."

The den was the section of the house that was below ground level. It was not in the official plans, and was created in January 2004 originally as a refuge from hurricanes. The family had to use it in September of that same year when hurricane Ivan, a category four monster, slammed into Grenada. In July 2005, a category one hurricane targeted Grenada again, leaving the Alexander clan grateful that they had put in this cellar.

In 2009, Junior converted the cellar into a den for recreation and storage. Now it was used more for storing stock for their electronics business. They also used it to store the merchandise that they got now and then from South America that they dared not put in the books. This section of the house was off limits to visitors. It was accessible only through a utility closet in the kitchen. Jeffrey was given strict instructions that he was not to bring his friends down there. He was allowed to bring girls to his room but he could not, under any circumstances, bring anyone to the den.

"So how much stuff those Vincy want?" Kellon began.

Kellon was the ever-present cousin of Junior and Jeffrey. He and Junior were only one year apart. They grew up together, attended the same primary and secondary schools, and while Junior was in Bogota, Colombia, on a Business Management scholarship, Kellon took care of Jeffrey. Kellon's mother was the older sister of John Alexander. When Kellon was born one year after Junior, John took him to live with them. Most people mistook them for brothers. They were both six feet five inches tall and muscular, and played on the national basketball team for a year. Only their hairstyles distinguished one from the other. They went almost everywhere together. They ran the family electronics business as a team. They attended sporting events together. And they conducted their side business as equal partners.

"Dem men say they want fifteen keys."

"We have enough for all that?"

"Yes, but I don't think we should give them so much. I say we give them ten."

"Good idea!"

"Cool. So how they getting it?" Junior did not relish putting drugs on one of their boats and going to St. Vincent. The risk was too great. Besides, the St. Vincent Coast Guard was very vigilant.

"They sending a boat. We suppose to meet them on Levera Beach on Wednesday night."

"Is a moonlight night. Dem men really like to take chances, *out*!"

Kellon shook his head as he thought about the meeting. He would have to arrange some additional security.

"Doh worry. I organising some extra protection," Kellon reassured his cousin.

"Great. But we don't want plenty fellas, eh. Can't bring attention to that operation."

Kellon grinned confidently. "Doh worry, man. I have somebody in mind."

Junior raised his left eyebrow. "One person?"

"Trust me, we secure. If dem Vincy try something, they dead." Kellon pulled out his smartphone and dialled a number.

Junior trusted Kellon with his life.

"OK. Let's go grab something to eat."

They headed up to the main floor as Kellon spoke into his phone in Spanish.

After they ate, the cousins returned to the den and spent just over one hour carefully packaging ten kilogrammes of cocaine for their rendezvous on Wednesday night.

# CHAPTER 3

**Base of the Special Services Unit**
**Point Salines, St. George's**

Inspector Andrews sat at his desk, his fingers a blur as they pounded the keyboard of his HP laptop. He was typing the December report for his commanding officer, Superintendent Jon Telesford, head of the DIA, while trying to listen to the evening TV news on GBN, the Grenada Broadcasting Network. Superintendent Telesford had his weekly Heads of Departments meeting with the Commissioner of Police on Wednesday.

The inspector was very troubled as he thought about the apparent increase in cocaine related crimes in the country over the past few months. The Coast Guard had intercepted four foreign speed boats on two different occasions trying to drop off drugs on isolated beaches in the south of the island. Not surprisingly, the occupants were South Americans. There were also the cases of five students from three secondary schools who were caught with packages of drugs in their possession. In one case, a school girl had the embarrassing situation of a small packet falling out of her underwear and sliding down her leg to the ground while she happened to be walking ahead of the school's vice-principal. Then there were the cases of three British women who were stopped and searched as they were about to board a flight to England. Two had ingested balls of cocaine and one had the drugs stuffed in a condom hidden in her rectum. Andrews shook his head sadly as he typed, wondering why people wouldn't seek other legal means to try to survive, instead of risking lengthy prison terms or even death. His head suddenly jerked away from the computer monitor and towards the TV, as the attractive female news anchor began a report about a girl found dead on the compound of a secondary school in St. Patrick's.

"*. . . there are unconfirmed reports that the student may have died from a drug overdose*," the anchor read from the teleprompter.

Andrews reached for the desk phone and dialled CID headquarters in the capital. He asked for Sergeant Roberts and was greeted by a gruff voice a few seconds after he was transferred to extension 403.

"Sergeant Roberts. How may I be of assistance?"

"Sergeant, this is Inspector Andrews, DIA."

"Inspector, I was just about to call you," Sergeant Roberts lied.

"Great minds think alike," Inspector Andrews pretended to believe him. He laughed silently.

"So what can I do for you, Inspector?"

"I just watching the news here. How all-you didn't call me about that child's death in St. Patrick's?" Andrews was a bit annoyed to be left out of the loop.

"Inspector, we just reach back down," Roberts started to explain.

"Man, I don't mean after you come back. Somebody from the DIA shoulda been on site with CID. You know that any suspicion of drugs at a crime scene and my people must be there!"

"Well we didn't really see drugs. Only some powder around the girl nostril."

"So you mean to tell me she was powdering her nose and she died?" Andrews' voice reeked with sarcasm.

"No, Sir. This powder was not like baby powder. We send a sample of the stuff for testing."

"How you know is not baby powder?"

"I was on the scene. And the principal told us she strongly suspect is cocaine."

"How she know that? She is an expert?"

"She was a nurse in England for plenty years. She say she seen deaths like that before."

"Oh, OK. I want to know the minute the results come back, what that substance is. How old was that girl?"

"Eighteen."

"What you know about her so far?"

"Well she has eight siblings and a mother. She was in Form Four."

"And you find out who was with her when she died?"

"Nope. But they tell us that two boys usually eat under the tree where she died. So we have to talk to them. Maybe they saw or know something."

"OK. Well lemme speak to your boss. He there?"

"No, Sir. ASP Sylvester left already. You could call him tomorrow."

"Alright. I'll speak to him tomorrow. We, departments, have to work together better."

Inspector Andrews hung up the phone, his mind working in overdrive. If that powder was indeed cocaine, that would make it drugs in four secondary schools that the police knew about. This time, a student was dead. He had a gut feeling that that particular incident was connected somehow to those fools in that orange house not too far from that school. Which drug dealer would paint their house bright orange anyway? But could these guys be so brazen to actually deal their stuff in a school in their own neighbourhood? He sighed. Gone are the days when the DIA spent much of its time uprooting marijuana trees and arresting people for having a couple of joints in their pockets. Now they had to deal with this evil called cocaine. He vowed that he and his team would put a big dent in the cocaine trade in Grenada.

# CHAPTER 4

**Wednesday January 16**
**Fort George, St. George's**

At 9:34 a.m., the door to the conference room of police headquarters at Fort George swung open and the six-foot frame of the Commissioner of Police strode through, followed by Deputy Commissioner Johnson David. The twelve men and three women who were seated around the large rectangular table all rose to acknowledge the presence of the superior officers in the room. These fifteen officers each headed a department in the RGPF. Only the Training School was not represented at today's meeting. They were all dressed in their khaki uniforms, the appropriate insignias identifying them as superintendents or assistant superintendents. Everyone stared at the glaring face of the commissioner, noting the impeccably pressed khaki uniform, spit-shined shoes, and socks pulled up to just below the knees. They stifled smiles, knowing that she never liked being late and was obviously annoyed at her own tardiness. No doubt, the European tourists milling around the fort this morning had delayed her for a few minutes, probably to take pictures with Grenada's highest ranking police officer, or maybe even to ask questions about the fort itself.

The commissioner scanned the faces of the top minds of law enforcement gathered in the room, and relaxed a bit. She mustered a faint smile as she greeted the officers who sat down after she and her deputy took their seats at the head of the table. She knew that some of the men were not pleased when she landed the position a year ago. The women were elated when history was made in the country as she became Grenada's first female police commissioner. But no matter their opinion on her appointment as Commissioner of Police, she was very qualified for the position.

Commissioner Katherine Coutain née Stephen was a Grenadian by birth, but grew up in England. She emigrated at the age of three with her parents and two brothers in 1965 and settled in East London. Her family had worked hard to get their children into the best primary and secondary schools they could afford. By the age of nineteen, she had already passed her Cambridge GCE A' Level exams in Law, English Literature, Sociology and Psychology. She joined the Metropolitan Police Force in London three years later. Her diligence, intelligence and attitude guided her steadily up the ranks of the force. She became a Chief Inspector by the age of thirty-three and five years later she was a Chief Superintendent At the age of forty-two, the now-married mother of two teenage boys had become Operational Command Unit Commander of Homicide and Serious Crimes. She was responsible for over one thousand personnel in London who investigated murders and other serious crimes. In 2006, Commander Coutain began thinking about returning to her native Grenada to retire at some point. In 2009, she became Deputy Assistant Commissioner in the Metropolitan Police Services. Two years later, she resigned her post to take up the vacant position of Police Commissioner of the Royal Grenada Police Force. She had killed two birds with one stone: returning to Grenada to live, and continuing her dream career as a police officer, the rank of Police Commissioner being the icing on the cake.

Commissioner Coutain made a few remarks about the importance of tolerating the visitors outside then asked Superintendent Jennifer James, the head of the Financial Intelligence Unit to say a word of prayer. The meeting then got down to business. The commissioner informed the officers that they would be focusing on preparations for Independence Day celebrations as well as the fight against the illegal drug trade. She nodded to Superintendent Telesford of the DIA who rose to present his report on the activities of his department.

Telesford presented a thorough report with the aid of a Power Point slideshow of graphs and statistics, and still-photos of apprehended suspects. There were also videos showing drug busts and surveillance of suspects. Everyone listened and watched attentively, some taking notes, others nodding or grunting from time to time. At the end of the fourteen-minute presentation, he downed an entire one-and-a-half litre bottle of spring water and sat back in his chair, waiting for questions and comments.

The silence in the room was deafening as the officers pondered the serious nature of the drug trafficking business in the country. Commissioner Coutain inhaled and exhaled deeply and audibly. She sat up, leaned forward and put her elbows on the table. Sixteen pairs of eyes bored into her expectantly as if an immediate solution to the drug problem was imminent. They waited for that sultry British accent to massage their ears.

"What we have just seen troubles me immensely," she began. "We cannot and will not allow our beautiful country to be overrun by these greedy and selfish drug barons. Who are the main people in the trade?"

"We're looking at the Alexander boys in Sauteurs," Superintendent Telesford replied. "But there is another family in Woburn we have to keep an eye on as well."

"You mean the Johnson family?" Assistant Superintendent Clive Sylvester asked. He was the head of the CID and knew a bit about the Johnsons who lived in Woburn, on the southeast coast of Grenada.

"Yes, dem self," Telesford nodded at Sylvester. "But we only hearing about them doing bad things. No proof. No witnesses. Just like the Alexanders. Those people very smart, man." The exasperation was obvious in his voice.

Commissioner Coutain wasn't pleased with Telesford's last statement.

"This is unacceptable. Criminals can't be smarter than us. What do we know about the Alexanders?"

Telesford pulled out a folder from his briefcase.

"Well, Junior and Kellon Alexander are cousins. Junior and his younger brother inherited a fortune from their father when he died. Now they own that big house on High Street in Sauteurs. They also have a couple of boats, some farmland and three apartment complexes."

Low whistles echoed in the room as the officers realised the extent of the Alexander's assets. Superintendent Telesford nodded his head in agreement with their amazement.

"Yes," he continued, "they own a lot of stuff for some young fellas. They also own that electronics store in Grand Anse."

"You mean Universal Electronics?" Superintendent James inquired. Six months ago, she was appointed head of the FIU, the department charged with investigating financial crimes including money laundering.

"Yep. They sell phones, computers, TV'S and other electronics."

Commissioner Coutain grunted. She turned to Superintendent James.

"Is there any indication that those boys are dealing with funny money?"

"No, Ma'am. So far everything looks legit. Those fellas have their money spread out in so many areas it would be hard to track if they were washing dirty money."

"But not impossible," the commissioner retorted. "I've seen cases in London where people were caught in the least expected ways." She looked directly at Superintendent James.

"I want you to dig deeply into the finances of those Alexander blokes. If they bought a snowcone yesterday, I want to know. I want to know how they've been spending their money for the last five years. I want to know their tax history."

Superintendent James sighed quietly. "Yes, Commissioner."

"And please do the same thing for that Johnson family also."

Superintendent James looked up sharply, mouth half-opened, as if to protest. She held her tongue and nodded curtly to acknowledge the order. Eleven months ago, the commissioner did promise all department heads that it wouldn't be business as usual, so she shouldn't be shocked that she was given this mammoth task. But her department had only seven investigators.

Commission Coutain stood up. The officers gave her their full attention.

"Officers, we have to get a handle on this drug trade. I don't recall seeing our streets and villages flooded with crack and cocaine addicts. So it means the drugs are being shipped out of the country. We just saw some pictures of women hiding drugs inside their bodies. I was always embarrassed to hear about West Indians caught at Gatwick with balls of drugs in their stomachs or in some other orifice. We don't want our country to be known as the Isle of White Spice. It seems that we have a war on our hands. Our economy depends on how successful we are in this battle. We will win this war! I want all hands on board."

The firmness in the commissioner's voice gave the other officers a huge boost of confidence. Some even felt like applauding but knew it would be inappropriate.

"So this is how we will start," she continued. "We will patrol our waters diligently. I know we have eight boats in the Coast Guard. How many are currently operational, Superintendent Clifford?"

The commander of the Coast Guard Unit responded on cue.

"Ma'am, we have six boats working right now. And remember, we have the newest and best cutter in the region, the latest Damen Stan patrol boat. Everybody respect the *Victoria*."

"Great. We have to use our boats for more than just search and rescue. I know how hard it is to patrol our coastline and our islets. But we will have to do something to deter delivery of drugs by boat. The South American boats are very fast. Can ours keep up?"

"Yes," Superintendent Clifford reassured Commissioner Coutain. "The two new 33-feet Defender Interceptor boats could deal with any fast boat those drugmen want to come with. Each boat has three Mercury 300 outboard engines. Those babies real fast. And we could patrol far out to sea. The cabins have a/c so our fellas will be working in comfort. Doh worry. The Americans train our fellas real good!"

Coutain smiled at Superintendent Clifford's excitement. The man's face was lit up, his eyes wide as a child who had just received his desired Christmas gift. His rate of speech had increased to the extent that she had to force herself to pick out the more important words of his soliloquy in order for her to understand what he was saying.

"And what happens if they shoot at us? Those people are well-armed, aren't they?"

"Our boats are equipped with machine guns, Commissioner. Our people are well trained. They will deal with any threat to our maritime security."

"Good!"

Commissioner Coutain looked around the room at each solemn face. She cleared her throat.

"Ladies and Gentlemen, I am serious about taking the battle to the drug traffickers. Under my watch, Grenada will *not* become the Isle of White Spice. We shall intercept and confiscate all cocaine shipments that pass through our waters and prosecute the traffickers to the fullest extent of the law. And we mustn't forget the fight against marijuana trafficking also. But this cocaine business is a serious threat to our security and our economy. I expect results. All departments must be on board in this war. The Prosecution Department must be ready to put the squeeze on these criminals. The Rapid Response Unit has to be ready for war, literally. Those people will not hesitate to defend their interest with deadly force. So we must reciprocate with even deadlier force. I want you to conduct operations regularly, Superintendent Duncan, in conjunction with the

Drug Interdiction Agency. Do not give any suspected drug trafficker or dealer time to relax."

Superintendent Jimmy Duncan, the Head of the RRU, was a veteran of Operation Urgent Fury in October 1983 when the Americans led an invasion force into Grenada. He was a 17-year old soldier of the People's Revolutionary Army back then, battling American Navy SEALS who were attempting to rescue the Governor General who was holed up in his mansion protected and surrounded by dozens of Grenadian army troops. The SEAL team had surprisingly found itself in a tough battle, but superior training and better equipment gave them the edge. The young Duncan had escaped in the bushes behind the mansion after possibly killing two SEALs. He later joined the RGPF, in 1988. Now at the age of 47, the career military man sometimes accompanied his men on joint drug raids with DS-2 or DS-3 to ganja farms in the mountains. He loved the thrill of these moments.

He regarded the commissioner with steely eyes. "Commissioner, we will turn up all ants nests in this war. I know people will start to complain about their rights, but as long as we have your full support, we will conduct our mission without fear or favour. Those drugmen don't stand a chance."

"Oh shit!" Superintendent Alice Mason of Immigrations quipped. "I sorry for dem drug fellas."

"Damn right!" Superintendent Levy Grant of the SSU almost shouted. "My people ready to take it to those slackers."

Commissioner Coutain nodded, a satisfied look crossing her face. If there was a legacy she wanted to leave behind when she retired, it would be that she severely crippled the illicit drug trade. It seemed like she had the full backing of the police hierarchy. Now it was time to move forward. Well, first she had to hold discussions with the prime minister who was also Minister of National Security.

The commissioner suddenly lifted her head as if she had just remembered something.

"I say, what's up with that child's death in Sauteurs on Monday?"

ASP Sylvester filled in the group on the incident at the St. Patrick's Secondary School and where the investigation was at the moment.

"So we're trying to find out who was with the girl last. Some children reported that the spot where she was found is the usual spot where two boys eat their lunch."

"Have we found those boys yet?" the Commissioner asked.

"We have a name. An Alexander boy."

"Alexander again? Would this one be related to the suspected drugmen?"

"Possibly. Alexander is a very popular name in St. Patrick's. Tomorrow my detectives are going up there to check out a few things."

"OK. Good work, everyone."

The commissioner turned the meeting over to Deputy Commissioner David who began a discussion with the Police Band Leader and the head of the Artisan Squad on continuing preparations for the February seventh independence celebrations.

Almost five hours later, the officers began filing out of the meeting to head to their various offices around the country. Superintendent Telesford called Inspector Andrews from his cellphone to begin consultations on the plan of action of the DIA.

# CHAPTER 5

**Thursday January 17**
**1:30 a.m.**
**Levera Beach, St. Patrick's**

Kellon Alexander sat on an overturned wooden rowboat on Levera Beach, inhaling the salty air as a brisk breeze blew around him. He gazed offshore to the north at the almost perfect cone that was Levera Island that rose out of the Atlantic Ocean. The offshore island, commonly called Sugar Loaf, was only one mile directly across from his position on the mainland. He was always fascinated by this geographical feature that was part of the volcanic chain of islands that made up the Windward Islands. The cone rose about two hundred and fifty metres above sea level and cast a shadow in the moonlight on the waters towards Levera Beach. He hoped they would still have some moonlight when those Vincy fellas showed up. Those guys must be crazy to navigate the waters and rocks between St. Vincent and Grenada at night just to pick up some cocaine on this isolated beach on the northeastern tip of the Spice Isle.

Kellon was accompanied by a five-foot-one-inch muscleman aptly nicknamed Shortman. What Shortman lacked in height he made up for in strength. He was one of a few enforcers that Kellon and Junior used from time-to-time to do some extraordinary jobs. Shortman had seen his fair share of battles, and a scar running along his right cheek from temple to chin attested to that fact. Even his bald head appeared to have gone through some muscle building. He had dropped out of secondary school in Form Four after he was accused of sexually harassing several female students and a couple of female teachers. Hardly anyone messed with Shortman. He had once picked up a bus driver who had cursed him about his mother, and tossed the big-belly man into his own windshield. Two armed police constables who were coincidentally on the scene ran away in terror but returned with six officers as backup to detain the short strongman. *No one messed with Shortman!*

The two men discussed the plan. Junior had dropped them off at the isolated beach thirty minutes earlier and returned to Bathway Beach about two miles aback to wait. He was using an old Suzuki Escudo for this run. He couldn't use his X-Trail in a drug deal and risk being identified by inquisitive people. If the exchange happened without incident, Kellon would call his cousin to pick them up. If there were problems, they were to hike back to the village of Plains using backroad tracks and wait for a pick up. They couldn't have a car with them at Levera Beach and take the chance of being trapped in here, as there was only one road between this beach and Bathway. A coded message would be sent to Junior by text to let him know the status of the exchange.

Both men were armed and dressed totally in black. Even their socks and underpants were black. Kellon had a Glock 30 on his left hip tucked into his belt. The semi-automatic pistol fired .45 calibre rounds from a ten-round magazine. He always loved how the gun felt in his hands whenever he fired it on the shooting range at the old Pearls airport. Shortman had an AK-47 Kalashnikov rifle slung over his right shoulder. This very weapon had seen action in October 1983 when his uncle was a soldier in the PRA fighting the invading Americans. Uncle Bonds had often boasted of shooting down a Blackhawk helicopter with the rifle, but Shortman highly doubted that. He cleaned it regularly, ensuring that the Russian-made assault rifle could efficiently fire its 7.62 mm rounds. He checked the metallic curved magazine for the hundredth time. Kellon glared at him as he snapped the magazine back into place.

"You want to wake up everybody?" Kellon hissed.

"Man, you see anybody else here?" Shortman snapped back.

The beach was devoid of any human activity. They were surprised that people weren't walking around on the beach trying to glimpse endangered leatherback turtles digging nests to lay eggs. Turtle-watching was a very popular activity on this beach.

"What's that?" Kellon pointed to Shortman's neck at something that was glinting in the moonlight.

"Shit! Is only my chain," Shortman replied sheepishly. He took off the silver chain and tucked it into his pocket.

"OK. Stay sharp. Dem fellas should be here anytime soon."

"We shoulda really have more men," Shortman grumbled.

"Don't worry. We covered."

"If you say so." Shortman was unconvinced. He caressed his rifle and smiled in the moonlight. If those fools try anything, is lead in their tail, he thought. He was being paid $500 to babysit Kellon tonight. The Alexander cousins had also agreed to pay him an additional $1000 if he had to shoot anyone. He hoped he had to shoot somebody. He thought about what he would do with the money. Perhaps now he could buy that Samsung phone he wanted so badly. Then more girls would be checking him. He grinned, a gold-capped incisor glinting in the moonlight.

Less than 150 metres to the east of Kellon and Shortman, a slim figure was concealed in the brush on the rocks overlooking the beach. Toni was the backup that Kellon was relying on tonight to provide extra cover in case the Vincentians double-crossed them. The 28-year old sharp-shooter was hired time and again by Kellon to provide security from afar. Tonight, she was sitting on the moist ground, looking through the Schmidt and Bender scope of her Parker-Hale M-85 sniper rifle. The weapon was fitted with a flash suppressor to prevent detection in the dark, and could send a 7.62 mm round slamming into a target 900 metres away. She hoped she wouldn't need all ten shots in her magazine. In fact, she hoped she wouldn't have to shoot anyone at all. She had no problems killing anyone who threatened Kellon. Apart from performing a duty for the $2000 she was paid for tonight's mission, she had deep feelings for the tall Grenadian. She munched on a Twix as she thought about love and family.

Born to a Grenadian father and a Cuban mother, Toni grew up in Cuba with her mother after the latter was shipped back to the communist island in 1983. Her mother was among hundreds of Cubans who worked on constructing Grenada's international airport. The Americans hadn't hesitated to send the construction worker back to Cuba even after she had proven that she was married to a Grenadian. Antonia Gabriela Diaz was born in March 1984 and never got to meet her dad. He had died in 2003, two years before she was able to come to Grenada to see her father's side of the family. She bonded well with the family and remained in the Spice Isle, becoming a citizen and getting a job as a Spanish teacher at a prestigious boys' secondary school in St. George's, in 2007. Who would have guessed that she was an enforcer and assassin by night? But the low teacher's salary just wasn't cutting it. So she had decided to put her military training to use. Fortunately, it was for someone she liked a lot. As she was thinking about the direction her life was taking, the monotonous and rhythmic crashing of the waves on the rocks below threatened to hypnotise her to sleep. A low purring coming from the direction of the waters offshore brought her mind to full alert. She swung the M-85 around and peered through the scope until she made out the shadow of a moving craft. It was a cigarette with three figures aboard. The Vincentians were here!

# CHAPTER 6

Kellon and Shortman heard the purring of an outboard engine long before they were able to discern the shadow of a speedboat bobbing in the waves offshore. The boat had no running lights. It appeared to be one of those fast twelve-foot fiberglass cigarettes that are popular in Grenada, St. Vincent, and the Grenadine islands. Kellon could make out three figures in the boat. He pulled out a small flashlight and signalled to the craft.

"Get ready," he said to Shortman. "Be alert!"

"No problem." Shortman swung his AK-47 so that the muzzle was facing forward and down. He clicked the safety off. He tried to relax as much as possible.

Kellon switched off the safety on his Glock. He hoped he didn't shoot himself in the leg. He remembered Plaxico Burress, the American NFL player who was thrown in prison after shooting himself in the leg. He laughed softly in the wind.

The men watched intently as the pilot guided the boat towards them. Whoever was at the wheel seemed to be quite skilled. The pilot brought the bow of the sleek green and yellow craft just up to the shoreline, and a tall black figure carrying backpacks jumped off and waded to shore. As the man walked through the breaking waves towards the Grenadians, he seemed to be drifting slightly to the east, or right of them, and not directly between the boat and the welcome party. Kellon and Shortman exchanged puzzled looks. They couldn't recall the sea current running from west to east at this beach. If the current was affecting his movement at all, the visitor should be moving slightly to the left of them, in a westerly direction.

"Hey, what's up, Blackie?" Kellon called out to the Vincentian who was now standing on dry land about six metres away. He knew the man from previous dealings. People often thought that he was called Blackie because of his very dark complexion. Even his palms were almost the same colour as his very dark skin. But his name was actually Blackie – Deron Blackie.

Blackie wasn't wasting time in small chat. "You have the stuff?"

Kellon nodded to Shortman to move forward.

"Look it here," the bald Grenadian yelled. "You have the money?"

Blackie held out two bulging backpacks. They contained one million dollars. This wasn't the movies so there was no briefcase of money. He imagined the things he could do with this money. He was paid $2000 to drop all this money off and pick up some drugs! He shook his head as he thought about the situation. He could easily have taken the one million, given $5000 to each of the men in the boat, and gone to another island to live happily ever after.

"Look it," he shouted at Kellon. He threw the bags a few metres in front of him towards the waiting men. Shortman walked towards him with his own cocaine-filled backpack.

Kellon kept an eye on the boat as it bobbed up and down in the breaking surf. The pilot was revving the engine now and then, trying to keep the boat in the same general spot. The third man was standing as best as he could in the rocking boat, holding on with one hand while clutching a semi-automatic rifle with the other.

Shortman handed his backpack to Blackie then turned to pick up the money. As he took a step back towards Kellon with the payment, he heard a command from Blackie and froze.

"Wait! Don't move!" came the husky voice of the Vincentian.

Kellon could not believe his eyes and ears. He pulled out his Glock and held it against his right leg.

"Blackie, what you doing?"

"Shut up! Change of plans."

Blackie was now pointing a pistol at Shortman. "Bring back the money!"

By now, Shortman was very furious. This Vincy boy was actually pointing a gun at him!

"Take it easy, Shortman," Kellon pleaded. "Just give him the money back."

"Blackie, what you doing?" shouted the gunman in the cigarette. "You know we come just to collect the coke and drop the money. Don't cause trouble."

"Man, they always takin' advantage of us. I tired risk me life for Missah Jones, ello. This time we gettin' paid for real."

"You will never get away with this," Kellon warned.

"Oh really?" Blackie snorted. "How Missah Jones will know after we kill all-you? We keepin' the money for we-self and bringin' the coke for . . ."

Blackie's head exploded as the report of a high-powered rifle reached everyone on the beach, and his body pitched forward a couple metres. Shortman was almost blinded by the flying grey matter from Blackie's brain. The already enraged man screamed in alarm. He brought up his automatic rifle and rotated his body toward the boat, searching for a target. By that time, the pilot was moving the boat toward his fallen comrade while the third man had a good bead on an exposed Shortman and squeezed the trigger of his weapon. Metallic messengers of mayhem moved menacingly towards Shortman, stitching the muscleman diagonally from right shoulder to left hip. The sound of the impact of the bullets on his muscular body was sickening. His face contorted in a combination of pain, rage and fear. He managed to squeeze the trigger of his AK-47 before he fell forward on his face, his intestines spilling into in the shallow surf.

By this time, Kellon had opened up with his Glock, emptying his magazine in the direction of the boat. He thrust his pistol forward with each shot as if that motion would make the projectiles travel with greater velocity to their intended target. Not a single bullet came close to the craft. He swore in rage, and raced towards his fallen friend. The bloody water and spilled guts told him Shortman was dead. He retched a few times. Another shot rang out and the gun-toting Vincentian on the boat toppled dead overboard, a 7.62 mm round having carved a destructive path in his upper chest cavity before exiting his back. Kellon dove to the ground and started crawling to the rowboat higher up on the shore. He was shaking with fear and anger. The mission was in tatters. He started screaming. He heard a third shot from the sniper rifle and the boat engine sputtered and died. The pilot jumped overboard, his right arm useless after it was hit by a round from Shortman's AK-47. He began swimming north towards Levera Island, propelling his body forward with his left arm while kicking furiously. Kellon doubted the man could make it in the very strong undercurrent out there. He pulled out his phone and texted Junior with trembling fingers: BRKN ARW.

In the mansions on the cliff above the beach, lights started to come on. Two minutes later, calls began flooding into 911 describing automatic gunfire and muzzle flashes on Levera Beach in St. Patrick's. By then, Kellon was beating a hasty retreat away from the scene, leaving the drugs and the money to the waves. He jogged two miles back to Bathway beach intending to turn inland to cut through Levera Development for the village of Plains. He was grateful that he was an experienced long-distance runner and kept up his training every week. He knew Junior had left Bathway beach as soon as he got the text. He hoped Toni was also hoofing it to her cottage in the Bathway development area. He owed her big time for saving his life. As he jogged up the concrete road entering Levera Development, flashing lights pierced the dark night. He ducked behind a tree as a police car raced along the Bathway road, obviously on the way to check out what was going on at Levera Beach. Damn, the Sauteurs cops responded very quickly, he thought. Shouldn't they be in the station watching wrestling or something? As soon as the car disappeared in the distance, he got up and practically sprinted the rest of the way to rendezvous with Junior in Plains.

# CHAPTER 7

About fifty minutes after the gunfight on Levera Beach, four dark blue Isuzu D-Max double-cab pickups rolled through the village of River Sallee on their way to Levera Beach. Each vehicle had the letters RRU emblazoned across the sides and held eight personnel of the Rapid Response Unit, besides the driver, armed to the teeth and ready for action. The last pickup in the convoy, Team Four, stopped at the bridge that separated River Sallee from the Bathway and Levera section of St. Patrick's. Six men and two women poured out and set up a roadblock to check every vehicle that would attempt to leave, and to prevent anyone from getting into the area. They were all dressed in black combat fatigues and boots and each carried a Colt M4 Carbine assault rifle. Each person also had a 9 mm Beretta tucked into a hip holster and a black KABAR Night Raider knife in a sheath strapped to a thigh. The females wore black BDU caps while the men secured black Boonie hats on their heads with thin straps under their chins. Sergeant Bishop was the officer in charge of this team and after three minutes he radioed the convoy ahead to report that the checkpoint was set up.

The convoy stopped at the final corner about 100 metres before Levera Beach, and everyone except the drivers alighted. Inspector Taylor and his group of seven men of Team One split into two groups of four. Each group took one side of the gravel road to remain in the shadows and to avoid making excessive noise in the still night. They were outfitted with the same gear as Team Four. They jogged towards the beach, two arms-lengths apart, crouching as they went so as to create as small a target as possible. For three full minutes they observed the beach from the treeline that separated the sandy soil of the beach from the gravel soil of the land.

*But wey dem men from Sauteurs Police Station*, Inspector Taylor wondered. He was told to expect four men waiting for them. He shrugged then called up Team Two. He directed Constable Victor from that team, with his M60E3 Light Machine Gun, to the cliff on the east side of the beach to provide cover for everyone on the beach. The constable headed silently to the same general area that Toni Diaz had occupied about an hour earlier. He found a comfortable spot, and radioed the inspector when he was set up.

Team Three, led by Sergeant David Reeves, moved up to the treeline in another five minutes. They took up positions facing the bushes and the road from which they came. Then Reeves called up the vehicles. Team Two covered the first team while Inspector Taylor and his men crawled across the sand to get closer to the objects that were being tossed about on the shoreline further down the beach.

Taylor determined that there was no immediate threat to his men at the point where there appeared to be a couple of dead bodies. He ordered Team Two to patrol the rest of the beach to the west and secure the entire area. Ten minutes later, a voice in his ear piece told him the beach was secure. He pulled out a cellphone and called CID, the Central Police Station, and Inspector Andrews of DS-1. He was relieved that Andrews was already in St. Patrick's on his way to the crime scene, and that four detectives from the CID were passing through the checkpoint manned by Team Four. Obviously, the 911 officer on duty had made the right calls. He expected the officer on duty at Central to call the relevant superior officers. This situation called for the direct attention of the commissioner, her deputies and Superintendent Telesford of the DIA.

The patrol boat *Levera* of the Grenada Coast Guard left its base in Carriacou, Grenada's largest dependency, at 3:40 a.m. The officer in charge of the base was ordered to dispatch the US-built Dauntless-class boat to patrol the waters off St. Patrick's. Its mission was to look for and intercept any craft coming from Grenada and travelling north. The mission was classified hot, so all five crewmembers were armed, and the 12.7 mm machine gun was set up on the forward deck. The forty-foot boat cruised south at close to twenty-two knots. The sea was relatively calm with waves less than five feet, and the moonlight made it easier for the crewmen to scan the waters ahead of them. They headed directly to the area outside of Sauteurs, St. Patrick's, then turned east towards Levera where the waters became choppier. They were two miles off Levera Beach within thirty minutes after leaving Carriacou, and were surprised to see a lot of activity on the beach. Chief Lewis established radio contact with the party on the beach and spoke with Inspector Taylor.

"Inspector, we didn't meet any boats on the way down. What we looking for?"

"It look like there was a drop-off on this beach. So look for a speedboat of some kind. Maybe a cigarette."

"OK. We going and check around Levera Island. I doubt they might try to go south down the Atlantic side of the mainland."

"You never know. But check around Levera still. I think another boat coming up from main base to help out." The Coast Guard Command was sending one of its new Interceptor boats from the main base in True Blue on the south side of the island.

"Ten-Four!"

The *Levera* headed off to the other side of Levera Island. Chief Lewis smiled to himself as it dawned on him that he was about to patrol around the island that lent its name to his boat.

"Stay alert, men! We don't want to be ambushed by anybody."

No one responded, but the clenched jaws and intense stares out the windows betrayed how tense the men were.

# CHAPTER 8

**3:50 a.m.**
**Sauteurs, St. Patrick's**

Kellon sat in the basement of the Alexander mansion shaking uncontrollably. Junior was trying to console him but he kept shaking his head as if trying to get rid of the image of Shortman's intestines lying in the Levera surf. He cursed over and over, muttering to himself about what he would have done to Blackie if Toni hadn't shot that Vincentian "badman" in the head.

"That *pendejo* lucky he dead!" Kellon suddenly yelled out. "I woulda kill him with my bare hands."

"Take it easy, Cuz," Junior tried to calm him.

Kellon breathed deeply. "Man, you wasn't there to see Shortman guts on the ground. I shoulda really hold ah automatic instead of this small piece." He threw his empty Glock against a wall in rage.

After Junior had received the text that the mission was a failure, he had left Bathway immediately and sped to Plains. The plan was for Kellon and Shortman to hoof it to this village via back routes in the event that something went wrong and they had to avoid the main road. But he had never expected a shootout and the death of three men, including Shortman. He didn't care that the Vincentians were killed, but Shortman's death was a huge blow. He had really liked having the muscleman around him, especially when he was walking through the town of Sauteurs. If Shortman was with him and he accidentally stepped on a man's foot, the man would quickly apologise for placing his own foot under Junior's. He shook his head sadly as he thought about the eight-month old baby that Shortman had just had with a girl from Marli. What was he going to tell this woman? He picked up his phone to make a call to St. Vincent. After three rings, a high-pitched voice answered.

"Jones."

"Mr. Jones, Alexander. Grenada." Junior always had to resist the urge to laugh whenever he heard Dexter Jones' voice. He had never met the man, but was told that the Vincy was a massive six feet eight inches tall, and weighed about 290 pounds. How could a man who was practically a giant have such a tiny voice?

"OK. What is the problem?"

"So your men decided to go into business for themselves?"

"What you mean?"

Junior could hear Jones breathing heavily as if he was about to have a heart attack. He could also hear quivering in the man's voice.

"Blackie tried to rob us, man. Now he and dem men dead."

There was silence for almost one minute. Only the heavy breathing told Junior that Jones was still on the line.

"So you take me money?"

"Man, we lost our drugs and the money." Junior could feel the anger rising as he thought about the gunfight as Kellon had described it. "And one of my men is dead."

"Look, man, I real sorry. So all my people dead?"

"Nah. The man driving the boat took off swimming."

"Man, stop making joke. How he could swim from there to here?"

"I really don't know. But he jump off the boat. Maybe he drowned or reach one of dem rocks offshore."

"Shit! Man, that is a million dollars I lost. You better get back my money."

"Really? So was our fault your man got greedy? If you want your money go on Levera Beach for it. But leave my merchandise for me if you see it there."

"You mean to say you so stupid to leave the stuff and the money on the beach? All-you really stupid down in Grenada!"

"Look here, Jones, *your* man tried to rob us and kill us and now you disrespecting me on the phone!"

Dexter Jones took a deep breath to calm himself. These Grenadian fellas just came on the scene and they want to play expert. He was in this business for over twenty years. He was running marijuana and money between Grenada and St. Vincent for that entire period, and started getting into cocaine three years ago. He knew some people in Grenada who could help him get even with these Alexander idiot-boys.

"OK, Alexander," he said quietly, "is not your fault. But if I find out you set this up, your whole family dead."

The last statement was loud enough for Kellon to hear. He grabbed the cell from Junior's hand and yelled into it.

"You playing real bad from over there, you *maricón*. Your people killed my friend. I holding you responsible. You better watch your back."

Kellon pressed the end button on the touchscreen to terminate the call, leaving Dexter Jones in his secure mansion in Kingstown, St. Vincent, staring at his own Blackberry in disbelief.

Junior looked at Kellon and sighed.

"You know, you shouldn't have done that. Now we could have a war with that stupid Vincy."

"Yeah. Well is his men that cause all this trouble so is his fault."

There was a moment of silence as the cousins thought about the ramifications of a drug war between Jones in St. Vincent, and them.

"Boy, you sure the police won't connect us to that stuff?" Junior asked anxiously.

Kellon cocked his head to one side and thought for a moment.

"Nah, man. That bag we used is an old bag from long time. And I sure they can't connect us to the coke. And nobody else was on the beach."

Junior heaved a sigh of relief. This was the first time that one of their exchanges had gone bad. It wouldn't be a good thing to be caught right now. He and Kellon were known as upstanding citizens of the parish of St. Patrick's. Every Christmas, they provided food hampers to many families in Sauteurs, Marli and La Fortune. They often donated stationery and school supplies at the end of August to children in their community. Junior was even thinking about running to represent St. Patrick's west constituency in a future national poll.

"Well, the only thing that could connect us to that scene is Shortman," Kellon continued quietly. "Everybody know he is we boy."

Junior shook his head in sorrow once again and Kellon went to the back of the den to strip his Glock and clean it. He left it disassembled on a table in the corner. Then the cousins retired to their respective rooms to try to get some shut-eye. They had lost a major fortune tonight. Neither Alexander got a single minute of sleep as they both thought about the one million dollars they had just lost.

# CHAPTER 9

**6:30 p.m.**
**Sauteurs, St. Patrick's**

Kellon and Junior sat on the black leather couch in their huge living room impatient for the 6:30 evening news to begin on channel six. The talk of the town and throughout the country was the shootout on Levera Beach last night. They hadn't heard anyone mention their names as having being a part of that incident; at least not directly. The entire town of Sauteurs knew that Shortman was killed. Some were sympathetic, while others expressed the opinion that he deserved to die that way given the life of violence he had lived. There were whispers in the town that he was probably on a mission for the Alexander cousins. Everyone knew that he worked for them. What could he possibly be doing on a beach alone with a million dollars and so much drugs? Nobody dealt with that kind of money in St. Patrick's except the Alexanders of High Street.

The introduction to the evening news began, and Kellon turned up the volume on their TV. Jeff walked in with a cheese sandwich in one hand and a bottle of malt in the other.

"Boy, you ain't tired eat?" Kellon needled him.

"This body needs food if I have to play football in *La Liga*," Jeff replied, chuckling.

"Yeah right," Junior muttered. "And I will be the next Governor General of Grenada."

They all laughed then stopped abruptly as the news anchor came on and started reading the headlines. They weren't surprised when the top story was the shootout on Levera Beach. The young lady read a fairly accurate account of what was found on the beach hours after the shootout. They showed video of the place flooded with black-clothed RRU officers, and CID detectives. Kellon also recognised a few members of DS-1. The camera panned to show a Coast Guard Defender-class Interceptor boat towing a cigarette slowly towards the beach, the sunlight glinting off the glass and the silver surface of the 33-foot naval craft.

"There's the commissioner," Jeff suddenly shouted above the voice of the news anchor.

Commissioner Coutain was striding around wearing a camouflaged BDU complete with camouflaged cap and a sidearm. The video showed her being flanked by the Head of the DIA, and followed two steps behind by three heavily armed personnel of the SSU, including a female officer.

"She think she so good," Junior said. "She come back to Grenada to clean up the place."

He and Kellon snickered. The anchor then introduced some comments made by the commissioner and the video switched to a press conference that she had hastily called earlier that afternoon. This time she was dressed in her official commissioner's khaki uniform. Her jacket was covered with a row of award ribbons making her look like a heroic soldier. Two high ranking officers of the RGPF sat on either side of her.

"Well, I think she real hot," Jeff remarked.

Kellon and Junior exchanged looks.

"Boy, hush your mouth so we could hear what she saying," Kellon said gruffly, backhanding his young cousin playfully.

The commissioner was describing the scene at the beach that morning as was reported by Inspector Taylor of the RRU when he had first arrived there with his men. She offered a theory that this may have been a drug deal gone bad between Grenadians and

Vincentians. The police had discovered that the disabled boat was from St. Vincent. She also reported that the Coast Guard had fished a body from the water just off Ronde Island a few miles north of Levera beach. She went on about the police force working hard to eradicate the scourge of illegal drug use and drug trafficking in Grenada, and that her force cannot sit idly by and let the island become the Isle of White Spice.

"She is good," Jeff commented.

Junior and Kellon kept exchanging glances after each point the commissioner made. She was disclosing some of the plans the police had for the fight against drug trafficking, especially the cocaine trade. Apparently, she intended to work closer with the Trinidad and St. Vincent Coast Guard units. This could put a dent in their plans. Trinidad had a very well-equipped Coast Guard Unit with very fast patrol boats, and aircraft.

"Well, is now dem drug squad will be all over the place," Junior muttered.

"For real," Kellon agreed. "Look out for patrols by all the squads. And all the Coast Guard boats will be out at sea more regularly."

"Well, all those fellas were doing was watching TV anyway," Jeff said, shaking his head. "I never see a police force so lazy yet."

"Boy, what you know about the police force?" Junior said to his brother. "We have to respect what those guys are doing. We can't have dem Vincy fellas coming down here and making trouble."

Kellon nodded solemnly in agreement. Jeff got up to go to his room to look at an NBA game on his TV. After he disappeared down the hallway and his room door slammed shut, Kellon and Junior began a whispered discussion about what they would do next. They had already moved their stash of cocaine from the den to the basement of their apartment complex in Frequente in the south of the island. They figured that if the police made a connection between Shortman and them, they would search their Sauteurs home first. They always had a lawyer on speed dial for situations like these if the need arose.

"The Community Relations Department of the Force reported that one of the men killed was from Sauteurs. Is it true that he was an employee of a prominent family of Sauteurs, and if so, was he working for them at the time he got killed?" It was a question from a reporter working with one of the weekly newspapers.

Junior's head whirled around to look at the huge screen at the same time as Kellon's head popped up from reading a text on his cell phone.

The Commissioner hesitated for what seemed like hours before offering a response.

"Who asked that?" Junior's eyes were balls of fire.

"Not sure, but I think I recognise the voice," Kellon replied, his nostrils flaring. He was just as angry as Junior. Was someone implying that they were a part of that incident? To what other "prominent" family could she be referring? They were the only "prominent" family in Sauteurs and everyone knew that.

"Can we sue her?" Junior wondered aloud.

"We kyant even suggest that. She didn't call anybody name."

Commissioner Coutain chose her words carefully as she answered the reporter's question.

"First of all, this Shortman is from Sauteurs, and he was the only Grenadian we found on the beach. We cannot just make assumptions because we have been seeing people with other people. We can only work with the evidence found. It's not what you suspect or what you know. It's what you can prove. And right now, it appears that he was alone. If we find anything that connects him to anyone else, we'll act on it accordingly. But I implore you, the media, please do not report that we are looking at other people in this investigation. Because at this point, we're not."

What the commissioner didn't say was that they had found footprints alongside those belonging to Shortman higher up the beach close to an overturned rowboat. Someone else was definitely on the beach but nobody else was found alive or dead. The RRU did find evidence that someone had occupied a spot on the high ground on the east side overlooking the beach. When the sun had risen, Constable Victor had noticed two spent shells lying on the ground not too far from where he was positioned with his M60 machine gun. He had called for detectives to come to the spot to check it out. The two detectives found three shells which Inspector Taylor deduced had come from a sniper rifle. He had suggested to the detectives that the decapitated individual on the beach was most likely killed by a sniper. Commissioner Coutain wondered who could have such a weapon on the island.

The reporter was about to ask a follow-up question but the commissioner cut her off. Coutain thanked the pool of reporters assembled, then lifted her six-foot frame gracefully from the chair and marched out of the room. She was followed by her deputy commissioners.

The news anchor then switched to a segment about the Prime Minister's reaction to the shooting incident. He seemed angry, as if his country was invaded by a foreign army. He endorsed the comments made by Commissioner Coutain, promising to give her the full support of his government in her effort to rid Grenada of this "White Spice". He emphasised the importance of portraying the country as a safe tourist destination, where visitors could come to enjoy nature and leave with our natural spices.

"We cannot be known as a place where it's easy to ship or trans-ship drugs," he said into the camera. "Thirty, forty years ago, we didn't have to deal with this menace called cocaine. Only marijuana. Now we have to deal with both, as well as synthetic drugs. My fellow citizens, we are at war with these drug lords. They are a threat to society, to our people and our economy. And our nation will win this war. If you're a drug lord, we're coming for you. We will not rest until all of you are brought to justice."

The Prime Minister's tone was as cold as a January Grand Etang breeze, and the Alexander cousins shuddered in their living room as if frigid air had indeed blown out of the TV monitor. The man was serious! The gunfight had triggered a response in every section of society that they had never seen before. In a very rare instance, the government and the main opposition political party were agreeing publicly about something. Kellon and Junior were actually scared.

"Boy, let's hold up on all transactions until this thing cool off," Kellon suggested.

"We have one thing lined up, and that's it," Junior said.

"What you talking about?"

"That fella on the tourist boat should be coming by on Tuesday."

"Damn. That man trip is too routine. Anyone could figure out when he coming, and where exactly he going."

"Well, we already agreed about that pick up so we can't fall back on our word."

"Man! OK, but after that, we taking a break for a while."

The men listened to a few more stories making the news then switched channels to look at an NBA game. It was almost mid-season and the race was tight out in the Western Conference. They were both Lakers fans. But their minds were far from the Bulls/Lakers game showing on TV.

# CHAPTER 10

**8:10 p.m.**
**SSU Camp, Point Salines**

Inspector Andrews and sixteen members of DS-1 had just finished watching the TV news on GBN in their air-conditioned meeting room. They were excitedly discussing the shootout that occurred earlier that day on Levera Beach, and the evidence they had found. Never in the history of the DIA had so much cocaine been found in one location in Grenada. The implications worried Andrews a lot. But DS-1 was set up with just that scenario in mind.

In 1999, the Drug Interdiction Agency was split into three squads, with Drug Squad One being the largest team. This team had the unenviable task of stamping out the cocaine trade in Grenada. The government had become alarmed at the marked increase in cocaine boats caught in Grenada's waters, and was horrified to find out that there were local drug lords who engaged in the trade. These drug lords did not engage too much in selling cocaine to the local population but they found innovative ways to transport the white powder to the United States. Inevitably, the US Drug Enforcement Administration, the DEA, took notice of this, and urged their Department of State to negotiate with Grenada to do whatever was necessary to wipe out the illicit trade.

Inspector Andrews was one of the first members of the new DS-1 to undergo training with the DEA. He was already fluent in Spanish therefore he was taken to the jungles of South American countries to observe and sometimes take part in classified anti-drug-trafficking operations. He returned to Grenada to train other police officers specially selected for the squad. They all had to demonstrate excellent athletic prowess, great thinking and deductive skills, and good proficiency in a foreign language, preferably Spanish. They also had to be able to handle small arms and assault weapons with ease, and be at least capable of defending themselves in hand-to-hand combat. However, perhaps their biggest asset was their ability to blend in with the population. As such, most of them no longer wore uniforms after becoming members of DS-1.

Andrews had thirty men and women under his command in DS-1. Some were currently in the field at Maurice Bishop International Airport tracking drug mules, or working undercover. The undercover agents were acting as drug dealers or posing as messengers for drug dealers. The mission had changed from trying to catch the street dealers and users to trying to find the top men and putting them behind bars. This was no easy task as the drug lords covered themselves very well. There were often many layers between these "big men" and the street dealers which often led to the dealers getting caught but the "bosses" escaping the reaches of the law. Andrews and his team had decided that they would go after the bosses, even if it meant that the upper levels of society would be shaken. This strategy was endorsed by Commissioner Coutain herself.

The DS-1 leader muted the TV and everyone turned their attention to him. He was solemn as he read an inventory of the items found on Levera Beach: a backpack with ten kilogrammes of cocaine; two bags with a total of one million EC dollars; several 7.62 mm shell casings; an AK-47 rifle; several 9 mm shells; one 9 mm Beretta. There were also three dead bodies on the beach. One body was identified as Ian "Shortman" Licorish. The other two bodies were still not identified.

"What about the speedboat?" Corporal Peters asked. "It wasn't registered in Grenada."

"Nah, it's a Vincy boat," Inspector Andrews answered.

"Usually those Vincy deal in marijuana," Peters observed. "I wonder why they switched to coke?"

"The recession hit everybody hard," Corporal Robert Sam remarked. "I feel they want to make a quick money. That was a lot of drugs for a Vincy to buy at one time."

"So what you think happen there, Inspector?" a young constable named Anthony Black asked. "I mean, everybody left the drugs and money on the beach. Real weird, man."

Inspector Andrews rubbed his chin thoughtfully then offered an explanation.

"I was brainstorming with the men from CID. Those of you who were there saw some shoe prints close to the prints belonging to Shortman. I think somebody else was there on the beach. And the RRU fellas found some shells on the cliff on the east side. They said it had been recently ejected from a weapon."

"So you saying a sniper was there somewhere?" Corporal Peters asked.

Andrews nodded his head in the affirmative.

"I think that Vincy guy tried to rob Shortman," he continued. "And the sniper shot him. That was a really good shot. I mean the distance wasn't far, but at night that sniper had to be well-trained."

"You shoulda seen the result," Sergeant Nathaniel Jacob said. "The top of dah man head was gone."

Sergeant Jacob was one of three trained snipers in the DIA. He spent most of his free time reading about snipers and their missions. His favourite movie was *Sniper* with Tom Berenger and Billy Zane.

"Natto, boy, it must be you who would admire something like that!" Sergeant Salisha Charles groaned.

Jacob grinned broadly.

"The sarge is right," Andrews said. "There is someone out there who is very dangerous. Our entire Force has five highly trained snipers. Now we have evidence that someone out there is just as good."

"Natto, where were you between midnight and four a.m.?" Sergeant Charles teased Jacob, laughing.

Jacob was lost in his own world, thinking about a duel between himself and that sniper, just like the characters in his favourite movie. He crashed back to Earth when he heard the question.

"Girl, you better move," he responded, pushing Charles so hard she almost fell out of her chair. "But it would be nice to come up against that guy."

There was laughter around the room and several team members exchanged glances and rolled their eyes.

Corporal Peters said, "'Nice' the man say? You really crazy!"

"OK, back to business," Inspector Andrews brought some order back to the meeting. "I think Shortman was shot by a submachine gun from the direction of the sea. We found one in the shallow surf."

"The boat the Coast Guard brought back!" Peters blurted out, suddenly seeing the light.

"Yes, Corporal," Andrews confirmed. "It looks like the body floating close to the shore lower down the beach fell from the boat, perhaps after he was shot by the sniper after he shot Shortman. By the way, the engine of that cigarette was shot up also."

"Like Shortman had himself some good cover," Sergeant Jacob said.

"And it still wasn't enough," Charles contended. "Looks like he needed a full platoon."

"You really believe that man they found close to Ronde Island was trying to swim back to St. Vincent?" Sergeant Phillip Mark asked incredulously. "He was wounded too."

"I suppose he didn't want to get caught down here," Inspector Andrews replied.

"But who so stupid to leave all that money on the beach so?" Charles asked, shaking her head from side to side. "You know how much things I coulda do with all that money?"

Scattered laughter sounded in the room. But every man and woman seated in that room thought about how much easier their lives would be if they had even one percent of that amount of money in their bank accounts. A few agents sighed.

"I guess that missing person got real scared and buss it," Peters suggested.

"You could be right," Inspector Andrews agreed. "Especially if the person was with Shortman. Would you stick around if you see your friend guts spilled like that?"

"That AK was under Shortman's body and still in his hand. I feel the other person had a weapon also," Charles remarked. She was one of eight DS-1 agents who were at the scene.

"Yes, true. The CID men found some shells on the beach that didn't match any of the weapons they found," Andrews told the group. "They think it came from a 9 mm."

"But, Inspector, you said they found a 9 mm pistol," a voice from the back shouted.

"These shells were found on the beach. The nine mill was in the water close to the body of the headless man."

"Well, CID have a big job of finding the gun those shells came from. A lot of people have 9 mm handguns," Peters said hopelessly.

"Well, they hoping there were witnesses. After all, it was moonlight," Andrews tried to sound hopeful.

"The RRU didn't meet a single soul on Bathway neither on Levera," Charles reported. "And the people in the house on the cliff were no help at all."

"We'll test the drugs and see if we could trace it somehow to somebody," Andrews said. "We doing that tomorrow."

The inspector discussed with the group how they would proceed in the next few weeks in this drug war. His squad was ordered to step up surveillance at the international airport and to follow any suspected mules whenever they entered the country. They wanted to see where they would lead the agents. DS-1 operatives would also join patrols at sea with the Coast Guard. Some members groaned inwardly because they dreaded riding on boats. But they all were excellent swimmers and divers. Their squad would be leading this war to eradicate White Spice from The Spice Isle.

# CHAPTER 11

Corporal Peters cleared her throat as she began her presentation to the assembled personnel of DS-1. She wanted to get this over with so that she could get home to watch *Burn Notice* on TV. It was already 9:10 p.m. Inspector Andrews had asked her to brief the team on the surveillance of Luis, a suspected drug trafficker working on one of the mega cruise ships that visited Grenada on Tuesdays. She and the inspector had taken pictures of the Hispanic-American, and they even had his fingerprints after he had used Andrews' camera to take a picture of a "loving West Indian couple".

Corporal Peters fired up a Dell laptop, pointed a remote control at the LED TV monitor, and brought up some photos of Luis taken at the Cruise Ship Terminal in St. George's. There were some chuckles as a few of the shots showed only a portion of Inspector's body with the American in focus in the background.

"Girl, they didn't teach you how to use a camera?" Sergeant Charles said to Peters.

The corporal grinned and continued with the slide show. There were a few pictures showing Luis in Sauteurs with the ever-present green backpack on his back. One scene showed him drinking a bottle of water as he stood by the doorway of a shop. Another showed him walking up Main Street. He seemed to be perspiring heavily in this shot as his t-shirt appeared to be stuck to his bulging pecks, soaked with sweat.

Corporal Peters then played a couple of short video clips. In the first clip, the foreigner was seated in the veranda of an orange mansion, looking northward at the ocean. The background noise suggested that the video was shot from inside a moving vehicle.

"You use a phone or a videocam for this shot?" Jacob asked. He was also an amateur photographer.

"The guys used a Sony handycam for this," Peters replied.

Another more shaky video showed Luis milling around at the front of the Esplanade Mall in St. George's. He appeared to be buying spices and t-shirts from vendors.

"Now I know that could never be a camcorder," Jacob concluded.

"Nah, that was my phone," Constable Michaels confirmed.

"So who is this guy, anyway?" Sergeant Charles asked.

Peters leafed through some papers in her folder before responding.

"OK. His name is Luis Felipe Ortega. He lives in Miami with a wife and two young children. Girls. This is his first season working on that ship. So that's one reason why we are wondering why he travels to Sauteurs everytime they visit our shores."

"He have a woman up there," Constable David Smith suggested confidently.

"Nah. He not even interacting with the girls up there," Peters said.

"Wha' happen? He racist?" Charles asked, a bit too contentiously. "Or maybe he gay."

"That's unlikely," Inspector Andrews replied. "Hispanics are usually friendly people. You didn't hear Corporal Peters say he married?"

"Well I know Hispanic men hardly letting a woman walk by without making a pass at her," Charles responded. "Wife or not, I sure he have other women."

"I guess whatever he doing up there is so serious he doesn't want to get distracted," Andrews said thoughtfully.

"So what do we do about him?" Jacob asked. "I mean, we should try to get that bag."

"Correct!" Andrews agreed. "Any ideas?"

That was what they loved about the inspector. He always wanted to get input from the entire team, from constables to sergeants.

"We could always have the officers at the security checkpoint in the cruise terminal check him," came a voice from the back.

All heads turned to look at the source of that deep voice. It was Corporal Redhead. He shrugged and continued.

"The police at that checkpoint hardly ever check the tourists and crew," he continued. "This could be one of those times when they decide to do random checks."

"Corporal, that's a good idea," Inspector Andrews said, nodding vigorously. He looked around the room to see others also nodding in approval of Redhead's idea. Some personnel mumbled in agreement.

"I'll talk to Immigration about doing random checks when the ship comes next week," Inspector Andrews said, making a note in his diary.

"So they should check him when he entering the country or when he going back on board?" Peters asked.

"I feel they should check him when he returning," Sergeant Charles said thoughtfully. "Let's see what he collecting up there in Sauteurs."

"Yes. I'll ask the fellas to check him as he going back on board," Andrews nodded in agreement.

Inspector Andrews was proud of his team. They had little to work with but they were willing to start with small ideas. Up to this point, they were running around catching small-time dealers. It was about time that they went after the big fish. Maybe they were on track to catch a tuna this year.

The team talked spiritedly for a few minutes about the shootout on Levera Beach, and the reaction by the prime minister. They knew they were in the frontline in the battle to get rid of White Spice from Grenada.

"OK, People, let's call it a night," Inspector Andrews declared. "Long day tomorrow. Good job, everyone!"

# CHAPTER 12

**Saturday February 2**
**Maurice Bishop International Airport**

Roland Johnson of the Security Department of the Maurice Bishop International Airport arrived forty minutes early as usual and parked his white Toyota Corolla in the staff parking lot. He got out and went to the trunk to remove his backpack. Anyone observing closely would have noticed that his small biceps bulged with the weight of the bag as he slung it over his shoulders. The backpack contained more than his lunch and the usual novel that morning. The predawn light was enough for anyone to notice his brown pants, cream shirt and security badge. He headed towards the security office in the main terminal building to clock in.

At 5:40 a.m., Supervisor Johnson began briefing the personnel under his command about the morning shift which ran from 6:00 a.m. to 2:00 p.m. Everyone wore the same colour uniform as the supervisor. Some of the middle aged female officers chose to wear skirts instead of pants. Their shift was to be a busy one. They were expecting nine flights during this shift: two internationals and seven regionals. One of the international flights was the American Airlines flight to Miami. The American carriers always demanded the stiffest of security measures which annoyed the security staff tremendously. The supervisor decided that he would personally deal with the scanning of checked luggage that morning, much to the surprise of some of his colleagues. Supervisors usually remained in the office or chose less demanding posts in the field for themselves. The personnel signed out hand radios and were dispatched to various locations around the airport to begin their duties precisely at six.

Johnson and a junior security officer headed to the baggage handling area to scan the dozens of pieces of luggage that were bound for Miami. He had his backpack on his back, and the junior officer, Matthew John, pointed out to him that it was against regulations to go to the secure areas with personal baggage. Johnson dismissed this by saying that he had a bowl with his breakfast in the bag and needed to eat it whenever he got a chance while they were scanning luggage. The young officer shrugged silently. The two men arrived at the security checkpoint. The supervisor greeted everyone boisterously, shaking hands and slapping some of the men on their backs, asking about family, and teasing them about who had fallen asleep during the night shift. This banter was customary among the personnel whenever they changed from night to morning shift. None of the men and women at the security checkpoint asked the senior security officer to put his backpack on the belt to run it through the X-ray machine.

Security Officer Johnson and his charge got to the baggage handling area and were met by two burly baggage handlers. The handlers started feeding luggage into the scanner as soon as suitcases, bags and boxes began arriving on the conveyor belt from the check-in counter. Johnson and his subordinate officer stared at the monitor, looking for anything that seemed even remotely suspicious in the X-ray images. A few times, they stopped the machine to consider some images, and they had to open nine suitcases to get a closer-look at suspicious-looking items. But in each case, the item was legitimate.

About an hour into the chore, Johnson ordered that everyone take a five-minute break. He asked John to get him a drink at the canteen located in the departure lounge. John sped off to get a bottle of Coke for his supervisor and some water for himself. The two baggage handlers strode out of the massive room, stretching and flexing their muscles. Johnson watched them disappear before springing into action.

The large blue suitcase was sitting with other pieces of luggage that had already being checked, cleared, and tagged. Johnson needed to remove the two packets of almost pure cocaine from his backpack and put them in that suitcase. He removed a big bowl of saltfish souse and coconut bakes and set it on the counter next to the monitors for the X-ray machine. Next he approached the blue suitcase carrying his backpack with the contraband and clandestinely transferred the items. About a minute later, Officer John returned to find his supervisor working up a sweat devouring his breakfast.

"Man, why you take so long?" Supervisor Johnson managed to ask between chews.

"I took less than three minutes, man," John replied. "Besides, there was ah line ah people there."

"Alright. Anyway, you reach back in time. You save me life," Johnson said, sounding relieved.

The burly baggage handlers returned and soon everyone was back on task scanning luggage. On one occasion, Johnson spent a few extra seconds at the section of cleared luggage as he closed and secured the large blue suitcase in which he had placed the cocaine. The special favour for his uncle was done.

Supervisor Johnson was commissioned by his uncle to get a few packets of cocaine through airport security onto a flight to Miami. He had been a supervisor for the past eight years, having spent a total of twenty-one years as a security officer at MBIA. This was a task he would normally refuse to do, but he needed the $8000 his uncle had offered. He needed to replace his car badly. He figured that he wasn't contributing to harming anyone – at least not in Grenada. All he had to do was place the stuff in a specially marked suitcase and it would be removed by someone in Miami who transferred luggage from the plane to the baggage handling facility at Terminal C of the Miami International Airport. The suitcase would later pass through US Customs without the drugs inside. He hoped he wouldn't have to do this again. Although he thought it was easy enough for him to bypass the security measures at MBIA, he didn't want to arouse suspicion by giving himself this assignment too often. He didn't want to lose his job, and he certainly didn't want to end up in prison for drug trafficking. He knew that his uncle was rich enough to probably get him out of jail. Uncle Johnson had a huge compound in Woburn, St. George's. He also owned several boats and cars. Apparently, business was very good for him. *Perhaps I should go into business with Uncle*, Roland Johnson thought.

The two security officers looked at the clock on the wall. It was 7:30 a.m. It was about time to start loading the jet. Right on cue, three more men came in and began loading the wagons with luggage to head out to the airplane. This flight was scheduled to leave at 8:50. Johnson hoped it would leave on time. The contact working at MIA finished his shift at one p.m. The three-and-a-half-hour flight to Miami left only a small window for any delay.

The American Airlines jet took off at 8:55 a.m. The Boeing 737 carried one hundred and fifty-eight passengers today. Supervisor Johnson heaved a quiet sigh of relief when he heard the jet leave. He texted his uncle that the plane had left on time and the special cargo was on board. He expected to see a deposit of $8000 in his bank account when he checked it online as soon as he got back to the office. He would use that money together with a $30,000 loan from a credit union to buy a new car. Well, a used, new car. He smiled as he pictured himself driving around in a second-hand Grand Vitara.

Johnson worked with junior officer John on luggage-scanning for another flight, this one a LIAT flight bound for St. Lucia, before he decided he'd had enough of this post. He radioed for a replacement and left with his backpack as soon as the young female officer arrived. He headed to the control tower to take up duty for the next two hours.

# CHAPTER 13

**Monday February 4**
**Maurice Bishop International Airport**

Supervisor Roland Johnson entered the office of the general manager of the MBIA at 12:55 p.m. for a one o'clock appointment. He had received a text that morning to attend an urgent meeting with the GM, Ramesh Ramsingh, and was urged to be on time. He couldn't think of any reason why the GM himself wanted to meet with him. Supervisors usually met with the Department Manager, and it was the latter who would meet with the GM. Maybe I'm getting a commendation for spotting those drug mules last week, he thought. He smiled to himself as he approached the GM's secretary. The young lady greeted him and waved him into Mr. Ramsingh's office.

Johnson entered the posh and spacious inner office with the smile still on his face, but it vanished in a flash when he saw six other people in the room besides the general manager. Fourteen eyes turned to appraise him. The GM was seated at one end of the large conference table, wearing a brown three-piece suit and a red tie. Johnson recognised Inspector Andrews and Sergeant Salisha Charles of DS-1, seated at the table to the left of Mr. Ramsingh. He often worked with them when they cased the airport looking for drug mules. His department manager, Brian Griffith, and junior security officer, Matthew John, were also seated on the same side of the table as the DS-1 agents. John seemed to be focused on something on the opposite wall. Judy Mason, the American Airlines country manager, and Marcia Belfon, the Human Resource Manager of MBIA, were in positions on the other side of the table. The only vacant seat was at the end directly opposite from Mr. Ramsingh. He headed for that spot.

"Afternoon," he greeted the group somewhat nervously.

Everyone replied in his or her own manner.

"Have a seat, Mr. Johnson," Ramsingh commanded.

Johnson took his seat and the GM cleared his throat. His black eyes drilled into the security officer as he began to address the gathering in his Trinidadian East Indian inflection. He cut right to the chase.

"Ladies and Gentlemen, we have two members of Drug Squad One with us this afternoon because somehow a quantity of cocaine managed to get past our security and make it to Miami on that American Airlines flight on Saturday."

There was only one AA flight on Saturday from Grenada, so everyone knew to which flight he was referring. Johnson's heart almost jumped through his throat, and he started sweating profusely.

"Needless to say, AA, MIA and the DEA are very mad at us here at MBIA for that security lapse. As you know, this is the second time in two years a quantity of drugs has made it to an American airport from here. To the Americans it looks like we have a problem with our security."

Mr. Ramsingh looked at the manager of the Security Department as he said this. Griffith shook his head in shame, inhaled and exhaled deeply.

"I will do a thorough investigation," Griffith assured the general manager. He turned to Johnson.

"Mr. Johnson, you were on duty with Mr. John here to scan the luggage going to Miami. Didn't you find anything during your scans?"

"No, Sir," Johnson replied quickly.

Sergeant Charles scribbled something on her notepad. She was the squad's psychologist. She was always studying people's behaviour.

"If that's the case, then there is only one other conclusion," Mr. Ramsingh said slowly. He didn't really want to accuse his employees of being drug traffickers.

"Hey, you accusing me of putting stuff in the luggage?" Johnson asked contentiously. "I sure the security video never show me doing that."

Inspector Andrews and Sergeant Charles exchanged glances. Charles made a note in her pad again, while the inspector stroked his goatee thoughtfully.

"What about you, Mr. John?" Griffith asked the junior security officer.

"Sir, I was looking at the monitor the whole time," John answered. "I didn't see anything like contraband. A few times, me and Mr. Johnson opened some suitcases but we didn't find nothing."

"The Miami office said the drugs were found in a sky blue suitcase," Mrs. Mason interjected.

Johnson gulped almost audibly. Damn! That was the suitcase he had put the stash in. What went wrong?

"You OK, Mr. Johnson?" Inspector Andrews asked him.

"Nah, yeah!" Johnson replied hurriedly. "I just really embarrassed that this happened on my watch."

"Mr. Johnson, why did you assign yourself to that area that morning," Griffith posed a valid question.

"Er, well, as you know, we want to have everyone experience all the different security spots around the airport. So since I didn't do that section in over a year, I thought I would do it that morning."

"Hmm," Griffith grunted as he looked at some documents. "It shows here that you did that section three months ago."

"Well it was so long ago I forgot when," Johnson said, laughing nervously. "Anyway, Mr. John and me was together on the post."

"Yes, about that," Griffith said. "Why did you send Mr. John away from the room?"

"I needed something to drink," Johnson replied.

The DS-1 agents were observing Johnson closely. The a/c in the room was quite low, yet Johnson hadn't stopped sweating from the time he entered. His lips remained parted as if a smile was stained permanently on his face. And he kept clasping and unclasping his hands. Sergeant Charles also noticed that he reacted suspiciously when the American Airlines country manager described the piece of luggage that held the drugs. But he wasn't in the video footage doing anything illegal as he scanned luggage.

"I feel all-you trying to accuse me of something," Johnson said to the general manager. "But look at the video. I didn't do anything. The most you could see me doing is eating some food inside there."

"Nobody is accusing you of anything, Mr. Johnson," Inspector Andrews reassured him. "We have to go with the evidence."

"Damn right!" Johnson exclaimed. "Nowhere in that security video all-you ever see me do anything illegal in there."

"Mr. Johnson, not once have you said you didn't put drugs on that plane," Sergeant Charles remarked.

Johnson looked at the sergeant and blinked.

"What you mean?" he asked puzzled. "But I telling you that all the time."

"Actually, she right," Griffith agreed. "You keep talking about you not on the video, but you never say you didn't put drugs on the plane."

Johnson thought about that for a few seconds. Damn! This wasn't supposed to happen! Somebody messed up in Miami.

"Look, I doh care what all-you say. I never put drugs in any bag to Miami and the security video proving that," he insisted.

Johnson's eyes suddenly lit up as he remembered the baggage handlers who put the luggage on the machine to be scanned.

"What about dem handlers," he suggested with a hint of desperation. "Is one ah dem who do it."

"They were within view of all cameras at all times," Griffith answered. "They never left their posts except when you called a break."

Johnson's downcast expression could have convicted him right then and there of the crime for which he was being investigated.

"Mr. Johnson, we noticed a $8000 deposit on your bank account," Inspector Andrews dropped a bomb. "What's that about?"

Johnson grabbed the arms of his chair so hard his fingernails dug into the wood. His mind was reeling. Prison in Grenada or prison in the States? Any evidence they have was circumstantial, he thought. He watched a lot of *Law and Order.*

"So you minding me business now?" he said to Andrews. "Listen, I done here. I want my union representative if you accusing me of trafficking drugs. I work here for over twenty years, man."

Griffith was shaking his head from side to side as he thought about the embarrassment his department had caused the MBIA and his country. The former police officer was all about honour and integrity, transparency and accountability.

Mr. Ramsingh looked at the HR Manager. She cleared her throat loudly, startling Johnson who had forgotten that she was also at the table.

"Mr. Johnson, we looked at the video footage and saw a few violations. You went to the baggage screening area with your bag. Mr. John told me he reminded you of that rule but you dismissed him."

Johnson glared at the junior security officer.

"As you passed through the passenger screening point, you didn't have your bag screened," she continued. "This is a blatant violation of one of our basic security rules. I'm very surprised that nobody at that station took your bag to screen it. They will all be disciplined appropriately."

Johnson sighed. His little deed had gotten quite a few people in trouble. This would be a black mark on his otherwise spotless record. Twenty-one years of service to the airport seem to be dishonourably heading down the drain. As he sat there listening to Mrs. Belfon, he contemplated resigning his position. But that could make him look guilty. He knew they couldn't prove anything without the video footage.

"So, Mr. Johnson," Marcia Belfon concluded, "as we conduct this investigation, we are going to place you on leave until we figure out where the breakdown occurred. As it stands now, you and Mr. John will take two weeks off with pay."

"What!" Johnson exclaimed. "You can't do that to me. After all I done for this airport?"

Inspector Andrews looked at Johnson scornfully.

"How come you not even interested in Mr. John's situation?" he asked Johnson. "I'm positive it was you who somehow got the drugs on board the plane. We just have to prove it."

"Man, you know me," Johnson rebutted. "We did some take-downs together. You know I won't do that."

"Money could make a man do anything," Andrews said.

"If you not careful with what you saying, I suing you," Johnson warned, wagging his right index finger in the direction of Inspector Andrews. "It have witnesses here who hearing you libel me."

"Mr. Johnson, calm down," Mr. Ramsingh tried to restore order in the room.

Matthew John seemed to be in a trance. He knew he was innocent of anything they were talking about. This was his third year on the job and he loved it. Now Mr. Johnson was putting him in this position. John looked at the ceiling and blew air out of his mouth in exasperation. He looked at his department manager who sighed when the latter returned the gaze.

Ramsingh addressed the room again.

"Ladies and Gentlemen, We will follow the lead of Mr. Andrews and his team as they investigate this case. Mr. Griffith, you will talk to your men before you dismiss them. Thank you, Mrs. Mason, for your contribution. And on behalf of the MBIA, I apologise for the security lapse. I will personally write to the administration of American Airlines to apologise. Grenada needs their service."

The GM stood and walked to the DS-1 agents to shake their hands. He thanked them for coming. He then escorted everyone except his HR Manager and the security manager out of the room.

Johnson and John headed silently to the security office to be interviewed separately by Inspector Andrews and Sergeant Charles. As they walked towards the office, they could feel stares burning into their backs. Nearly everyone working on the airport knew by now that they were suspects in a drug trafficking case.

# CHAPTER 14

**Tuesday April 16**
**10:40 a.m.**
**St. Patrick's Secondary School**

For the sixth time, Jeffrey Alexander read the note from the Principal that the head prefect had handed to him only a few minutes ago. What could Mrs. Sampson possibly want? He had a Math exam in less than half an hour. He hoped this wouldn't take long. He strode across the yard from the Form Five Block to the Administrative Building and checked in with the principal's secretary. The secretary ushered him into the inner office after speaking with her boss on the phone for a few seconds.

As soon as Jeffery entered Mrs. Sampson's office, his socks started to dampen with sweat. His feet would always sweat whenever he got nervous; it was a family trait. He knew the principal's office well because he was accustomed to being summoned to receive congratulatory messages after representing his school or his country at football. But this wasn't football season. His eyes fell on two men who were obviously policemen, but whose names he didn't know. He gulped.

"Good morning," Jeffery managed to say.

"Good morning, Jeffrey," replied Mrs. Sampson. "Come in. Stand by my desk here."

This time, it was Jeffrey's shirt collar that started to soak with sweat. Standing by the principal's desk was never a good sign! Could this be about Petisha's death?

Mrs. Sampson introduced the two visitors.

"This is Inspector Andrews, and Sergeant Roberts of CID."

Jeffrey stared at the officers while trying very hard to keep his knees from shaking.

"We investigating the death of Petisha Gilbert," Sergeant Roberts stated. "We hear that you were the last person to see her alive."

Jeffrey opened his eyes wide, trying to figure out how to respond. After what seemed like an eternity, he spoke up.

"I don't know, I leave her under the tree and went back to my class after I finish eat."

The policemen exchanged glances, causing Jeffrey to shift his stance. Mrs. Sampson produced a document resembling a chart. It was an attendance record sheet.

"Jeffrey, the records here say you were absent for the afternoon session on that day," the Principal pointed out. "Where were you?"

"Oh yes, I remember now," Jeffrey said, obviously making up as he went along. "I wasn't feeling good after eating lunch."

Sergeant Roberts grunted. "What you had for lunch?"

"Oil down we cook Sunday."

"So you weren't with Petisha just before she died?" the sergeant asked again.

"But ah just tell you I leave her an' go!" Jeffery snapped, irritated.

"Watch your tone, young man!" Mrs. Sampson warned.

"Sorry, Miss." Jeffrey's gaze dropped to his shoes.

Sergeant Roberts pulled out a translucent blue sports water bottle with the initials "J.A." marked with a black permanent marker at the bottom. He showed it to the visibly nervous student.

"This is yours?" Roberts asked, hoping that the boy would lie but wishing that he would not.

"Yes, I lost it some time ago."

"I see," the detective muttered pensively. He rifled through some notes in his file.

Taking up the baton, Inspector Andrews continued the interview.

"Jeffrey, did you give drugs to the girl?"

By now, Jeffrey's shirt was stuck to his upper body as perspiration was oozing from every pore. There was a pool of sweat on the Mrs. Sampson's desk where his right hand was resting. Three pairs of eyes were locked on him, as the adults waited with bated breaths for the star footballer's reply.

"I did not give that girl any drugs," he almost shouted, wagging his left forefinger in the air. "I don't know why you-all think I have something to do with her death. Where I getting cocaine from?"

Inspector Andrews raised an eyebrow. Sergeant Roberts' hands froze as he was leafing through notes. Mrs. Sampson peered at Jeffrey over her spectacles.

"Who said anything about cocaine?" Andrews asked rhetorically.

There was silence in the office for a tense few seconds before Jeffrey attempted to defend himself. He blinked a couple of times.

"All you trying to tie me up but I know my rights. I does watch *Law and Order: SVU.*"

Roberts groaned while Inspector Andrews rolled his eyes.

Mrs. Sampson chimed in, "Young man, not many students know that there are video cameras in a few spots around the compound. We have footage of you and Petisha at that spot below the tree just before she died."

Jeffrey was beginning to feel defeated. How could he refute video evidence? He looked at each face defiantly before launching into his final defence.

"That video could never show me doing anything to her. I really liked the girl. And like you said, Miss, the video show us together just before she died not when she died."

Jeffrey took a breath, pleased with himself that things were now going his way. As an avid fan of *Law and Order*, he knew how to defend himself from any head games these cops might bring. He was going to get away with this, and his brother would never know that he had pinched some coke and that stupid girl had snorted some of it leading to her death. It was her fault anyway. She killed her own self. He continued with his impromptu speech.

"Yes, she come and meet me and I give her piece of my lunch. I real sorry she died but I'm not responsible. I was trying to help the girl. Just ask my pardna, Andy. All-you trying to pin this on me because my brother rich. All-you just jealous. People always trying to keep a good man down." He made a show of shaking his head sadly.

Sergeant Roberts exchanged a look with Inspector Andrews and wished they had done this interview in the police station so that he could slap around this foolish prick a bit.

"Funny you should mention Andy," the CID detective said slyly. "He told us you give Petisha the drugs."

"Well how he could tell you that and he wasn't even there when she grab it from me!" Jeffrey's voice rose to a higher pitch, as the stress of the situation was taking its toll on him.

Again, silence permeated the room as the gravity of Jeffrey's statement sunk in. Only Jeffrey didn't realise what he had just said. He looked at everyone's stares with a puzzled expression.

"What?" he asked, bewildered.

"Jeffrey, we have to call your brother," Mrs. Sampson said solemnly. "He will have to meet you at the Sauteurs police station."

Sergeant Roberts sighed. He stood and addressed Jeffrey.

"Jeffrey Alexander, you are now a person of interest in the death of Petisha Gilbert. I sure the Drug Interdiction Agency also want to ask you some questions in their ongoing investigations as well."

Jeffrey's knees buckled and he would have collapsed to the floor were it not for the quick reflexes of Inspector Andrews. The DS-1 agent caught the student before he hit the floor and sat him on a chair. Principal Sampson produced some water for him to drink.

"Please don't take him away in handcuffs," the Principal pleaded with the officers.

A few minutes later, Jeffrey was riding in the back of an unmarked police car for the very short trip to the Sauteurs Police Station.

# CHAPTER 15

**3:45 p.m.**
**Sauteurs, St. Patrick's**

Luis walked slowly from the Alexander residence on High Street towards the bus stand half a mile away. It was a very hot afternoon, and less than a minute after leaving the orange mansion, he was sweating like a marathoner at the end of his race. His backpack was slung by only one strap on a shoulder this time. He knew that the back of his t-shirt would soak with sweat if he slung it entirely on his back. He didn't notice a barefoot teenager wearing cut-off jeans and a dirty green t-shirt following him on Main Street. As he passed by a vendor, he stopped to buy a coconut jelly. He always found the juice of the young coconut refreshing. He put the backpack on the ground by his feet so that he could fish out his wallet from a pocket at the back of his pants to pay the vendor. As he was dipping into his wallet, he caught a green blur in his peripheral vision. Before he could react, the teen who had been following him, snatched up the bag and sped off down Main Street in the direction of the bus stand and Sauteurs market.

The teenage boy was surprised at how heavy the bag was. Maybe it was clothes, he thought. He was already panting heavily under the weight of the backpack, after only forty metres. He began to wonder what was in the bag. He looked back to see the tourist racing after him, shouting in an unknown language. It definitely was not English.

Maybe he is a *payol*, the boy thought. The man then started shouting in English and was attracting attention from everyone on the street. Cars stopped, people ran out of shops, and a police constable joined in the chase of the delinquent boy. The boy decided to grab anything inside the bag, drop the bag itself and leave the area. He knew that many people in this town knew him, but he thought that once he dropped the bag, everyone would stop chasing him. He certainly didn't want that huge foreigner to catch him.

Luis was running with one hundred percent effort to try to catch the thief. That *ladrón*! He pictured his family being gunned down in their home in Miami. Shit! His daughters! He mustered some extra energy to run even faster. He had to get that bag back. He hoped that there was no policeman around. He wanted to catch that wretch himself. He wouldn't do anything to the boy. He simply wanted his load back without attracting any more attention. But it seemed like the entire town was involved in the chase, *including a policeman*. He groaned silently and thought about stopping. He was horrified to see the boy's hand disappearing into the bag. *Carajo*! Not good!

The teenager ran around a parked van and slammed at full speed into a six-foot-five-inch burly man talking on a cell phone. The skinny boy bounced off the man's sturdy body and landed on his back a few metres away in the middle of the street. The bag flew across the road and skidded into the drain on the other side. The item in the boy's hand disappeared under the van. He looked up at the reflective glasses that shielded the man's eyes. It was Inspector Charles, the man in charge of the Sauteurs Police station, and he was very pissed that his call to his only daughter was being interrupted.

He spoke into the phone, "Baby, lemme call you back."

"Daddy, what's happening there?" asked a concerned female voice from the other end.

"I'll call you later, *dou dou*." Inspector Charles ended the call.

Inspector regarded the boy sternly.

"Sammy, you making trouble again!" the plain-clothes inspector said matter-of-factly.

A crowd was now gathering. A constable ran up, his blue shirt soaked with sweat yet still tucked neatly into his black pants. Surprisingly, he was breathing evenly. Less than ten seconds later, Luis arrived. He took in the scene and spoke to the constable.

"Sir, I'll just take my bag and get back to my ship."

The constable, Regis, exchanged a glance with Inspector Charles. He turned to Luis.

"Sir, you have to come back with me to the police station to file a report about this incident."

"Is that really necessary?" Luis desperately wanted to get out of this situation. The sweat on his brow was now because of nervousness and not just from the afternoon heat. He noticed the big man watching him closely.

Constable Regis again looked at his commanding officer. This time the inspector spoke up, producing his police ID.

"Sir, I'm Inspector Charles of the Sauteurs Police Station. You have to come with us to make a statement. Constable Regis will carry your bag for you."

Luis realised that he couldn't escape this situation. He sighed.

"But I have to get back to the ship. We're supposed to leave soon," he tried to explain.

"Don't worry. You will make it back on time," Inspector Charles reassured him after checking his watch and noting that it wasn't yet four p.m. He knew that the ship was scheduled to leave at 8:00 p.m., and that all passengers were supposed to be on board an hour before departure.

Sammy was already in handcuffs. Constable Regis retrieved the bag from the drain across the road. It was open, and as he lifted it, a transparent plastic bag containing white powder fell out. The constable froze as he realised what might be in the parcel.

"Sir, come over here please!" he ordered Luis.

Luis took a few strides with heavy feet to reach the young police officer. He realised that his backpack was open and a five-kilogramme parcel of cocaine was lying on the road.

"This is your bag?" Constable Regis asked the American.

Luis hesitated. His mind was racing at a million miles an hour. Say yes, and it meant that the drugs were his and he would be arrested for possession and trafficking. Say no, and he would be found out later as witnesses may come forward to say they saw him carrying the bag. It was the same bag he had carried on the previous six visits to this town. He didn't see a way to get out of this one. He fumbled for words and his voice quivered as he responded to the question.

"Well, I. . . , not exactly. I mean, it belongs to someone I'm carrying it for back in the States."

"Hmm, we go figure this out in the station," Constable Regis decided. "Let's go."

A white pickup carrying two uniformed officers arrived from the Sauteurs Police Station, and Inspector Charles heaved the teenager into the tray. One officer jumped in to watch Sammy on the short drive back up Main Street to the station. The inspector ordered Luis to sit behind the front passenger seat. The other officer retrieved the parcel that had slid under the parked van when Sammy fell, and gave it to Inspector Charles who sat beside the driver of the pickup. Constable Regis joined the American in the rear seat, sitting behind the driver. The second officer who had arrived in the pickup, replaced Regis on patrol up and down Main Street. For one afternoon, the town of Sauteurs was not as boring as many people would think.

At the Sauteurs police station, Inspector Andrews stepped out of Inspector Charles' office after spending several hours analysing data from his interview with Jeffrey Alexander earlier that day. The little twit just would not confess where he got the cocaine from. Andrews was ticked off that Jeffrey kept reminding him that his brother and cousin were rich and could hire the best lawyers to get him out of any jam. And the boy kept bringing up his rights and referring to the *Law and Order* TV series.

That show is really messing up a lot of Grenadians, Andrews thought, shaking his head in amusement. In the end, he had to let Jeffrey go because of lack of evidence, and no witnesses.

The top Grenadian narc stood on the steps of the entrance to the station thinking about what he had accomplished so far. The sample of coke found on that girl's nose was the same type as the coke they had picked up on Levera beach some time ago. That most likely meant that they came from the same batch. Andrews had a feeling that Jeffrey had pinched some coke from his brother's stash to show off at school. He had to find Jeffrey's friend, the boy who usually ate lunch with the young Alexander. He heard that this boy was a good student so it shouldn't be too hard to get him to talk. But why had that girl sniffed the cocaine anyway? Was she trying to impress Jeffrey? Rumour had it that she had a thing for him. But so did every girl in the parish. After all, the boy was rich, and a national footballer on top of that. Andrews cursed under his breath as he thought of those foolish girls throwing themselves at Jeffrey, most likely for a phone or some KFC. He looked at the people passing in front of the station, some greeting him respectfully. Ah, life in the rural community! Two teenage girls walked by wearing short tight dresses and talking loudly. On the other side of the street, four Chinese men stood in front of a Chinese-owned variety store. He smiled as he recalled his recent stay in China.

Andrews had spent two months in China in a seminar for security personnel of several developing countries. The participants were treated very well by their hosts, and they had learnt a lot about how to deal with security matters. For a country with a population of billions, the crime rate was amazingly relatively low. The visiting personnel were exposed to various crime-fighting techniques. They had even learnt some kung fu. The inspector rubbed his left ribs absent-mindedly as he remembered being kicked in that spot by the officer from East Timor during a sparring session. He remembered how quickly the army Lieutenant from Zimbabwe had rushed over with great concern on her face, to see if he was OK. He had looked at the compassion in her eyes as she gazed down at him, and forgot all about the intense pain. From that moment, they had become very good friends. What a shame it couldn't be more! They both knew that it could've been a different relationship had they not been so deep into their respective careers. Besides, she was a widow, and she had expressed her desire to remain single, as she saw no need to be in another relationship at this stage in her life. He understood that, kinda. He sighed as he thought about how similar they were to each other. If only their countries were not so far apart. They could have visited each other, perhaps every year. But they were content to communicate by making full use of the available communication technology. Thank God for Whatsapp and Skype! I wonder if she would want to join our Force here in Grenada, he thought.

A white pickup screeched to a halt in front of the police station, snapping Inspector Andrews out of his reverie. He was surprised to see a constable jump out of the tray and lift out a handcuffed youth . He was even more shocked to see a sweaty constable open the back door of the double-cab and step out. A lot had been happening while he was holed up inside Inspector Charles' stuffy office! Inspector Charles himself stepped out of the vehicle and opened the back door to let out a foreigner. *It was the American Andrews and his squad were covertly investigating!*

"Andrews, boy, you not leaving here now, you know," Charles called out. "This could be a very long day."

Inspector Andrews groaned as he noticed the half-open bag that the constable was holding. He recognised parcels of white and realised that this could be the breakthrough he needed. But why did it have to happen today of all days? There was an important game on NBA TV tonight and he had hoped to catch every minute of it.

"So who is that?" Andrews pointed to the American.

Inspector Charles looked at the sullen Hispanic man. He grabbed him by the upper arm to direct him up the stairs into the station.

"This man was apparently carrying that bag full of what might be drugs," he replied.

"You don't say!" Inspector Andrews didn't seem too surprised.

Inspector Charles paused for a moment and looked at the DS-1 officer curiously. He then motioned for his colleague to follow him into the station. The procession of officers and suspects into the police station drew a lot of attention from the other personnel on duty. Inspector Andrews typed into his Nokia, texting his commanding officer about the latest development.

# CHAPTER 16

**Sauteurs Police Station**
**Sauteurs, St. Patrick's**

Luis couldn't believe that he was caught in this *pinche* country with drugs. He was even more furious as he thought about the way in which he was caught. He wished he could get his hands around the neck of that *puto* kid who had run off with his bag. This was supposed to be an easy deal. Now his family was in danger. He vowed that he wouldn't tell the cops who he was bringing the merchandise for. He hadn't even known for sure what was in the bag. He shivered as he imagined two cars driving by his home in Miami Shores one night and spraying it with bullets, leaving his wife and two daughters riddled with holes as they ate dinner or looked at television. Tears flowed down his face. He shivered at the thought, and also because of the very cold air in the windowless room where Inspector Charles and Constable Regis had left him. He hoped they would believe him when he says he didn't know what he was carrying. His teeth began to chatter and he started shivering violently. He looked up as the single door to the room opened and a slim man with a goatee entered.

Inspector Andrews raised an eyebrow in surprise as his eyes fell on the trembling Hispanic. With a single glance, he took in the bulging biceps protruding from a slightly damp, yellow Grenada souvenir T-shirt; the black eyes that seemed to be teary at the moment; the bald head and clean-shaven face. He noticed the white calf-length sports socks that disappeared into white tennis shoes, probably size fifteen. The anti-narcotics agent had to stifle a laugh as he observed that the muscular foreigner was wearing a pair of plaid fluorescent orange three-quarter pants.

"You okay, Man," Andrews asked the shaking Hispanic man.

"*Hombre*, why is the a/c so cold?"

Inspector Andrews chuckled. They sometimes turned the a/c down to about fifteen degrees Celsius whenever they interrogated a suspect. They hoped that would encourage the interviewee to make a speedy confession of whatever crimes were committed.

"Sorry, Sir, it's very hot outside. But you already know that."

Luis grunted in frustration.

"Would you like a blanket?" Andrews offered.

"I just want to get outta here and go back to my ship," Luis muttered.

"Soon," Andrews promised emptily. "I'm Inspector Andrews of the Drug Interdiction Agency." He placed a thick manila folder carefully on the table and took a seat facing Luis, the door at his back.

Luis was shocked to see his full name in black permanent marker written across the face of the folder. His eyes bulged even more when he realised how fat the folder was. How much do they know about me, he wondered.

"So is that like the DEA in the States?" Luis asked, a slight smirk on his lips.

Inspector Andrews opened the folder and pulled out a document with four pages stapled together. The first page appeared to have data about Luis. He read some of the information aloud, ignoring Luis' question.

"Luis Felipe Ortega, from Miami Shores, Miami, Florida. Age thirty-nine. Two daughters, ages four and seven. Wife, age thirty-four. I see you were in the Marines for a few years. And you started working on that cruise ship fourteen months ago."

The inspector looked up and stared intently at Luis.

"So why are you transporting drugs?"

Luis sighed. "Honestly, Inspector, I really didn't know it was drugs."

Inspector Andrews looked silently at Luis for a full minute without a hint of emotion. He grunted and returned to browsing through the folder. He slid the datasheet to one side to expose a photograph of Luis walking through Sauteurs. Luis could not hold back a gasp. Andrews exposed more photos, pretending to scrutinise them carefully, but allowing Luis to see that he had been under surveillance for a long time.

"So, Mr. Ortega, where did you pick up the drugs?"

"I told you I didn't know it was drugs!"

"Well where did you pick up what you didn't know was drugs?"

"Someone gave me a bag and I simply had to take it with me."

"Hmm." Andrews slid two pictures across the table to Luis. Both photos were taken the same day but at different times. He explained both shots to the now sweating Hispanic man.

"This one here was taken at about two p.m. That one was taken at five-twenty the same afternoon. Notice how you're holding the same bag before and after you came up here to Sauteurs. So did you pick up a bag here in Sauteurs?"

Luis looked at the floor to his left.

He said, "What I mean is someone gave me stuff. It's not my business what it was."

Inspector Andrews laughed. He was beginning to feel cold now.

"Excuse me for a minute. I'll be back."

Luis wondered what was so funny. He was disappointed that Inspector had taken the folder with him. But the officer didn't seem to notice that one photo had fallen out of the folder. Luis looked at it and almost fainted. It was a picture of him sitting in the veranda of the orange mansion. He rocked back in his chair, interlaced his fingers behind his head, and sighed. He imagined himself in a Grenadian prison for a few years. His heart began to race as he pictured himself being some black guy's wife. He had heard that these third world countries had prisons that were teeming with disease. *Carajo*! Then he remembered that he was an American citizen. He blew out air from his mouth in relief. The American government would never let him spend even a day in a Grenadian prison. He smiled. The smile disappeared when the door opened and Inspector Andrews re-entered with bottles of water.

"I'm sure you know that we know what you've been up to," the police officer said, sliding a bottle of water towards Luis.

"Inspector, all of that makes no difference," Luis said with renewed confidence. "I'm an American. I'll be out of here in no time." He smiled defiantly.

Inspector Andrews' laughter was colder than the air that was blasting from the a/c unit in the wall above the suspected drug trafficker.

"Mr. Ortega, you are suspected of trafficking about ten kilos of cocaine. Yet you're talking about walking free just because you're American?"

The inspector started applauding albeit sarcastically. He nodded towards the door.

"There's the door. You can go."

Luis looked puzzled. It would seem that this cop had gotten instructions to release him. He grinned and stood up. He stepped toward the door.

"Thank you for your hospitality, Inspector," he said. "I really enjoyed . . . "

"Sit your butt back down!" Inspector Andrews snapped. "Do you want to be shot for escaping lawful custody?"

Luis froze and turned around confused. Wasn't he just offered freedom? Can't these cops make up their minds? He dragged himself back to the chair he had most recently occupied.

Inspector Andrews was no longer smiling as he addressed the foreigner.

"For months we have been checking you out. Thank God for

this breakthrough today. You'll be charged with drug trafficking. But we'll go easy on you if you tell us where you got the stuff and who you're bringing it for."

Inspector Andrews needed the latter piece of information to give to the DEA office in Miami. The Miami agents were working on the theory that drugs were coming in from the Caribbean to one or even three of the major drug dealers in the city. But they didn't have concrete evidence and witnesses. Luis could provide the necessary information to take down these drug kingpins.

Luis sighed hopelessly. Privately, he bid his family goodbye and made up his mind to spend the next few years in Grenada, in prison. He looked at Inspector Andrews with empty eyes.

"Inspector, I confess. I have been running my own operation in Miami. This was going to be my last run and I was going to get out of the business."

Andrews was unimpressed. Someone or something was keeping this man from telling the truth. He knew of cases where druglords would threaten a mule's family to ensure that the person would continue to carry drugs for them. This seems to be a classic case.

"Is someone holding your family hostage?" the inspector asked Luis. "Why are you so scared?"

Luis gazed at the ceiling, tears flowing freely down both cheeks.

"You can't help me, Inspector."

On a whim, Andrews decided to throw out the first name of a purported Miami druglord that came to mind.

"Are you transporting drugs for El Caballo?"

Luis suddenly gripped the side of the table so hard that his tan knuckles became red as blood pooled under the skin in that area. He sat frozen with bulging eyes that were pregnant with fright. At the same time, a foul odour diffused throughout the twelve by eight-foot room causing Inspector Andrews to literally recoil from the table. Then Luis fainted, falling sideways from the chair and crashing onto the floor. Andrews ran out of the room coughing and gasping.

"Charles," he called out to the top officer of the Sauteurs Police Station. "You won't believe wha' just happen. The man faint and mess he-self, *oui*."

"No way!" Inspector Charles said incredulously, amidst scattered laughter from other police officers. He ordered that Luis be revived and cleaned up and ready to be transported to St. George's.

"So you get anything from him?" Charles asked Andrews.

Andrews nodded in the affirmative. He was still rubbing his nose as he tried to get rid of that foul scent.

"We'll charge him with possession and trafficking."

"You sure we could get that possession charge to stick?"

Andrews reassured his colleague, "That won't be a problem with that boy as a witness."

"I hope so," Charles didn't sound too convinced. "But that man has been getting drugs from here for months. I want that source sorted out."

"Yeah. We'll get a search warrant for the Alexander house this week."

Inspector Charles laughed and shook his head. Good luck on finding anything, he thought to himself. He then looked at Andrews and said, "Can you believe we had two breakthroughs on the same day?"

"We'll disguise the raid by doing other raids in the area at the same time," Andrews said, a plan taking shape in his mind. He looked at his watch.

"Charles, boy, I real burn. Lemme head back to town now. I leaving it up to you to make the relevant calls and sort out the prisoner."

Inspector Charles couldn't believe Andrews was leaving him to make calls and do paperwork. He thought about what his conversation would be like with the American embassy and the agency for the cruise ship. The man hadn't asked for a lawyer yet but he was sure the embassy would get one for him. He picked up his phone to call his daughter to cancel their movie night.

# CHAPTER 17

**Sunday April 21**
**5:35 a.m.**
**Sauteurs, St. Patrick's**

The 24-year old woman on Junior's back giggled as he ran along the beach. He was running so fast that her long Indian hair was flying in the wind, almost parallel to the sand below his feet. He could feel her sharp nipples poking his back through her bikini top. She was holding on for dear life, and he was loving it. He was grinning from ear to ear. Then for whatever reason she started poking him in the ribs. *That's odd*, he thought, *her arms are wrapped around my neck. So who's poking me?*

Agents Nathaniel Jacob and Anthony Black of DS-1 looked at the sleeping, smiling Junior Alexander and almost burst out laughing. Obviously he was dreaming. The smiling figure hadn't heard when the two agents had entered his room to take him to the living room where the rest of the people in the house were being detained. They were involved in an operation to execute a search warrant on the Sauteurs premises of the Alexanders to look for narcotics. Sergeant Jacob poked Junior again in the ribs with the muzzle of his M-16. This time Junior mumbled and used a hand to brush off the irritating object. Jacob poked harder, and the sleeping man opened his eyes in confusion. He saw two figures dressed in black combat fatigues, black Kevlar body armour, and black BDU caps with the acronym DS-1 in white on the front. He recoiled to the furthest corner of the large bed, emitting a scream in horror that almost caused Black to squeeze the trigger of his weapon. The stench of urine filled the room a few seconds later. Both agents instinctively brought up a hand to cover their noses.

"Big man like you still peeing bed?" Jacob mocked.

Junior glared at Jacob with pure hatred, privately cursing him and two generations of his descendants.

"What all-you doing here?" Junior finally found his voice. He was almost certain that the two agents could hear his heart pounding in his chest.

"We here to search the house and property," Sergeant Jacob answered. "Everybody else downstairs already."

"Man, like you could sleep through a war!" Agent Black scoffed. "All this noise and you still sound asleep!"

Junior suddenly realised that there was a lot of noise in the neighbourhood. Dogs were barking incessantly; villagers were shouting at DS-1 agents and SSU officers as the law enforcement personnel dragged unwilling people out of their houses to begin searching for illegal drugs. Both ends of High Street were blocked off by SSU personnel brandishing automatic rifles. A total of forty-five DS-1 and SSU officers were manning checkpoints or patrolling cautiously among the houses in the neighbourhood. So this is the Commissioner's war against White Spice, he thought.

Junior was surprised to see such a huge gathering in the living room. He exchanged a look with Kellon across the room, and was relieved to see that he was okay. The Cuban, Toni Diaz, was sitting close to Kellon on one of the sofas. Jeffrey was sitting on another sofa, and there was a girl holding on to his arm that Junior didn't recognise. He frowned at Jeffrey for having a girl stay overnight when he didn't know about it. Sitting on the floor beside Jeffery was Man-O, one of the men who looked after the massive grounds. His mouth was bloodied from receiving a boot to the jaw as he had unadvisedly reached for a cutlass after the lawmen had busted through the door of the shed where he was sleeping. His woman, a plump lady, was whimpering beside him. There were also the two live-in housekeepers, two young ladies in their mid-twenties, who were both sharing a chair.

Junior counted no less than eight law enforcement personnel standing at various points in the room. They all looked grim, with automatic rifles pointing towards the floor, but index fingers poised above triggers. He was ushered to the couch on which Kellon and Toni sat. He was very embarrassed after wetting himself earlier in bed, and had to spend five minutes cleaning up. He was also embarrassed as he realised that he was the only one who had had no female companionship the previous night. His thoughts were interrupted as Inspector Andrews strode in.

"I'm Inspector Andrews of the Drug Interdiction Agency," the anti-narcotics agent announced. "I have a warrant to search the entire premises: this main house, and every shed within the compound." He handed a document to Junior.

"Our lawyer is on his way," Kellon said sullenly. They always kept their lawyer on speed dial just for situations like this. He had placed the call as soon as the first DS-1 agents had barged into the house and identified themselves.

"Well that was quick," Andrews muttered.

The inspector issued orders for his people to begin to systematically search the house. He asked the Alexanders if they were storing narcotics on the premises to which he received an expected no. He then pulled out an iPad and played a video for them. They were surprised to see a large Hispanic man sitting in their veranda.

"Do you know this man?" Inspector Andrews asked, watching them closely.

"No!" came the response simultaneously. Neither Alexander had ever seen that man before.

"This man is in your veranda in the video," Inspector continued.

"How is it you don't know him?"

"Plenty people does stop by here while we not home," Junior offered an excuse. "How we suppose to know who everybody is?"

"This man was arrested with a bag full of coke moments after he left this house," the inspector spoke to everyone in general. "If anyone knows anything, you won't be arrested for conspiracy to traffic drugs."

Each Alexander and all their associates kept their eyes on the floor or gazed out the window at the choppy sea in the distance. No one responded to Inspector Andrews.

Andrews approached Jeffrey with the iPad.

"Young man, do you know this man?"

Jeffrey looked at the video for a few seconds and answered in the negative.

"That's interesting. He said you gave him some drugs," Andrews bluffed. "You know you and he were in the police station at the same time."

"What!" exclaimed Jeffrey. "That man lying. I never see he before. I don't know he!"

"If there are drugs in this house, we'll find it," Andrews said confidently. He pulled out his walkie-talkie and ordered for the drug-sniffing dogs to be brought in.

Junior and Kellon exchanged glances, glad that they had transferred their stash to another location some time ago. They had also thoroughly sanitised the place so that not a scent of cocaine remained. They were still pissed at Jeffery for taking some of their merchandise, and worse, for bringing it to school. For his part, Jeffery sighed in relief as he thought about how he had flushed the small amount of cocaine he had shown to his friend Andy. Everyone looked up as two black Labradors and their handlers entered the spacious room. The large dogs barked loudly and menacingly, causing Man-O's companion to scream.

"Watch, all-you just make sure dem dog doh bite me!" she shouted.

Each K-9 team took a floor of the two-storey mansion to conduct their inspection. Every room, closet, wardrobe, cupboard, suitcase, bag, container, drawer, shoe and receptacle was checked. There were a few false alarms, but after forty-eight minutes, the teams returned without finding any evidence that cocaine was even stored in the house.

"I know you have drugs somewhere," said a disappointed Inspector Andrews. "I know you trafficking in White Spice. We will hol' you one day."

Kellon smirked at the top drug enforcement agent. "If you say so," he retorted.

The smirk vanished when Corporal Peters bounded in holding a battered brown backpack.

"Inspector," she called out excitedly, "I think we found something. This was in the shed outside."

"Who this bag for?" Inspector Andrews demanded.

No one owned up.

"Sah, ah tink dah is Man-O bag," volunteered Man-O's plump lady friend.

"'Ooman, hush you mouth!" Man-O hissed at the woman.

Corporal Peters poured the contents from the bag onto the glass centre table. Among the items were a wallet, a packet of condoms, and a clear plastic bag containing a white powdery substance. The corporal opened the wallet and found a national ID card with a picture of Man-O. She handed it to Inspector Andrews. The inspector compared the picture with the scarred face glaring at the thick lady.

"That definitely is you," he said to Man-O. "You want to tell me that is not your drugs in the plastic dey?"

Man-O suddenly went berserk, stood up and made a lunge at Inspector Andrews, bellowing at the top of his lungs. The other security personnel in the room raised their rifles, pointing them at Man-O.

"Don't shoot!" yelled Andrews. He deftly stepped aside a second before Man-O got to him, bringing up a straightened and stiff right arm to execute a classic clothesline. It was as if the man had hit a wall as his upper chest slammed into the muscular outstretched arm of the police officer. His lower body continued to move forward even though his upper body had stopped moving for an instant. This resulted in Man-O's body flying backwards, his legs up in the air. He crashed heavily to the floor, the air knocked out of his lungs momentarily.

"Police brutality," Jeffrey's girl screamed.

Inspector Andrews shook his head in amusement and looked at the DS-1 agent who was holding a camcorder and recording everything that was taking place in the room. He ordered that Man-O be handcuffed and placed under arrest for assault on an officer and drug possession. Two officers rolled Man-O onto his stomach to handcuff him then took him outside. The group in the living room heard the delirium of the crowd outside increase as Man-O appeared and seemed a bit beaten up.

Inspector Andrews regarded the Alexander boys and addressed them.

"All-you lucky this time. But know that we watching you. We will be searching all of your properties, including your store in Frequente. We will find the drugs you hiding. I know you had something to do with that business on Levera Beach. Shortman is your boy so he had to be working for you that night."

"Inspector," Kellon responded, "you failed in your attempt to pin anything to us. Did your dogs find anything? This house clean, clean, clean. You looking at upstanding members of the community, but you want to discredit us."

Junior continued where his cousin left off.

"Look out for a lawsuit for defamation of character. You barge into our home, pull people out of bed. You know what damage you did to countless children in the neighbourhood?" Spit was flying out of the enraged man's mouth.

Andrews was just glad that they were recording the entire scene.

He didn't want to take any chances and be accused of using excessive force in the execution of their duties. He didn't bother to reply to the Alexanders. He ordered his people to move out. As they were leaving the compound, he recognized the well-known attorney from St. George's, Denis Dominique. He rolled his eyes. *I should have known it would be him*, he thought. He and the lawyer locked eyes for a few seconds as they passed each other.

A disappointed DS-1 team left Sauteurs just before 8:30 a.m. without netting the haul they were expecting from the Alexander home. The four grams of powder they confiscated in Man-O's bag did little to console their pride. The operation had also netted a few joints of marijuana from some homes in the area. Four people were detained in all, and not one of them was the big catch of Kellon or Junior Alexander.

# CHAPTER 18

**Friday May 24**
**4:13 p.m.**
**Ten miles off Grenada's SE coast**

The Coast Guard Cutter *Victoria* punched through the six-and-a-half foot waves of the Atlantic Ocean at twelve knots as it headed on a northward course towards the town of Grenville, St. Andrew's. The grey, one hundred and fifty-four-foot Damen Stan 4207 vessel was on routine patrol as part of Grenada's war on White Spice. Sergeant Jerry Aberdeen of the RGPF sat in the captain's chair smiling to himself as he thought about how deserving he was to be given command of Grenada's newest patrol boat. *Victoria* was the flagship of the Grenada Coast Guard, replacing *Tyrell Bay* which was decommissioned a few years ago. He listened in admiration to the rumble of the two powerful Caterpillar engines that pushed the boat through the relatively turbulent waters off Grenada's east coast.

Aberdeen was a veteran of the Grenada Coast Guard with over twenty years of service to maritime security in Grenada. He recalled his secondary school days in the 1980's when he and a schoolmate would admire *Tyrell Bay*, Grenada's first coast guard cutter. They had vowed to be a part of the *Tyrell Bay* crew one day. Both he and that friend had eventually joined the RGPF in 1991, with Aberdeen opting for the Coast Guard Unit. His friend had disappeared into the ranks of the Special Services Unit. He was fortunate to be stationed on *Tyrell Bay*, and remained with that boat until he was promoted to second-in-command in the early 2000's. He was on that cutter when it had fought a famous battle with two Venezuelan pirate boats about twelve nautical miles southeast of Point Salines. The pirates had been regularly terrorising Grenadian cargo schooners plying the Grenada-Trinidad route. On that fateful day, the pirates had severely underestimated *Tyrell Bay* and its capabilities.

Aberdeen and his captain had used tactics and manoeuvres to combat the pirates that resulted in the sinking of one Venezuelan boat. The other boat sustained heavy damage and had to be towed to the Coast Guard Base in True Blue. Two Venezuelans lost their lives in the battle. The other eight men were incarcerated at Her Majesty's Prison in Richmond Hill, St. George's, for sixteen years. The Grenadian patrol boat had sustained some damage to its superstructure. Sergeant Aberdeen rubbed the left side of his face where a scar remained as a reminder of that sea battle. The tactics used then were still being used by Caribbean Coast Guard units during their exercises.

Inspector Andrews looked at his old schoolmate curiously, wondering why he was smiling. It couldn't be the slight rising and falling of the boat as it sliced through the waves; Aberdeen was used to these types of waters. They had both joined the RGPF at the same time, but he had preferred dry ground and was posted to the SSU while Aberdeen chose a career on the seas. Almost a couple decades later, Andrews was fighting drug trafficking as a member of the DIA. Today, he had decided to take up his friend's offer to ride along on a routine patrol of Grenada's east coast. He didn't particularly like the rough Atlantic waters, but he loved to look at the country's coastline from the sea on that side of the island. He absent-mindedly tugged at the clasps of his red life-jacket for the eighth time, and pulled the straps tighter. Everyone on board wore life-jackets as per regulations.

"Man, wha' happen to you?" he asked the smiling Aberdeen.

"Huh?" *Victoria's* captain blinked twice as if he was just regaining consciousness. "Nah, I was just remembering something." He laughed.

Andrews laughed also. "You ain't tired dream? You commanding your own boat now, you know."

Aberdeen stood up and stretched lazily. So far, their voyage had been uneventful as were most of their patrols. Occasionally, they were called to tow a fishing boat to Grenville after it had run out of fuel, or its engine had broken down. They didn't expect to encounter anything of significance since nearly everyone knew that *Victoria* wasn't a boat to challenge. They once had an run-in with a Vincentian speedboat as they were bringing the police band to Carriacou for a gig. The occupants of the speedboat had suddenly and inexplicably opened fire with automatic rifles on the patrol boat. Both crafts were about three miles outside of Hillsborough, the main town of Carriacou. Two crew members of *Victoria* were ordered to return fire with the Browning .50 calibre machine gun. Only one of the three men aboard the Vincy speedboat survived the onslaught from *Victoria.* Since that time, every boatman in Grenada and St. Vincent, and indeed the region, knew not to mess with the new flagship of the Grenada Coast Guard.

The sergeant brought his high-powered binoculars to his eyes and directed them to Grenada's shoreline on his port side. They had just passed Hog Island, Woburn, and Calivigny Island, and Fort Jeudy in the distance was now in his scope. He always admired the jagged cliffs that framed Grenada's east coast. But there were so many inlets along this coastline that he imagined the number of drop-off points for contraband just on this side of the island alone. His boat was too big to patrol most of them. He left those missions up to the Coast Guard's thirty-three-foot Defender class Interceptor boats. His role in this war on drug-trafficking was to intercept vessels that brought their dangerous merchandise to Grenada to be transhipped to metropolitan cities in North America and Europe. He lowered the binoculars and looked around the pilothouse, admiring the members of his crew who were at their stations. They all wore light blue shirts tucked into navy blue pants. Every crewman wore a red life-jacket and a blue cap with the yellow inscription VICTORIA at the front. He could hardly believe that he had twelve men under his command on this fast response cutter. He knew they were all ready to defend Grenada's borders at any cost.

The boat suddenly rose and fell as it crested an eight foot wave that caught the coxswain by surprise. Aberdeen grabbed his chair to retain his balance then looked at the sailor at the wheel with raised eyebrows.

"Sorry, Sir," the coxswain, Malik Patrice, said sheepishly. He was an experienced boatman from Petite Martinique, a small dependency of Grenada situated on the northeastern side of Carriacou. It was rumoured that boys from that tiny eight hundred acre island knew how to handle a boat even before they knew how to run. Patrice now had quite a task keeping the bow of *Victoria* aimed at the south-moving Atlantic rollers.

Aberdeen said, "Sailor, the sea getting too rough for you?"

Without taking his eyes off the sea in front of them, Patrice replied, "No, Sir. That one came from nowhere."

"Well use the instruments too," the captain said. "I ain't want to have to explain to the commissioner why I sink she boat."

"Sir, yes, Sir!"

"Captain, contact!" yelled the Second Officer, Joseph St. Paul. His binoculars were glued to his eyes as he looked northeastward. "Two O'clock."

Aberdeen scoped the patch of sea on their starboard side that his second in command had pointed out and was surprised to see a luxury yacht apparently adrift. The dark-blue sixty-foot craft bobbed idly in the water, its bow facing southward. The captain couldn't make out any movement on board. There was no anchor in the water. And there were no flags visible. It was just over three miles from their current position.

Aberdeen shouted to his XO, "You see movement over there?"

"No, Sir," St. Paul answered.

"I doh like this at all," Aberdeen grumbled.

"What's up?" Inspector Andrews inquired. He was also gazing in the direction of the blue motor yacht.

"What a luxury yacht doing out here on the Atlantic side of Grenada?" Aberdeen asked the DIA agent.

Andrews shrugged. He said, "Maybe they prefer the rough waters compared to the calm Caribbean Sea."

Aberdeen grunted, lost in thought. He decided to check out the craft. It looked like a very expensive boat too. He thought it was a Hatteras, a top-of-the-line type of motor yacht. He imagined a very posh interior. What might cause the occupants to abandon their boat? If they were sleeping inside they would've dropped anchor. And who drops anchor in this type of water anyway?

"Coxswain, change course to zero five zero! Take us over there, eight knots."

Patrice repeated the directive loudly then changed course to head towards the drifting blue boat. Red alert was sounded on *Victoria*. Sailors slung rifles over their shoulders, and the Weapons Control Officer plotted a firing solution in case they needed to use the main deck gun.

*Victoria* was outfitted with the Mk 38 Mod-2 25 mm Machine Gun System which could defend against any threat, rain or sun, calm or rough sea, day or night. They were over two miles away from the luxury boat, and if necessary the M242 chain gun could deliver a single round or multiple rounds of up to one hundred and eighty per minute, destroying the target. The 25 mm rounds would easily sink the fiberglass yacht from this distance if the captain decided there was an imminent threat to his patrol boat. The Weapons Control Officer had the advantage of a Toplite Fire Control System that included forward looking infrared radar, low light level television camera and a laser range finder. As *Victoria* gradually closed the gap towards the target, Aberdeen radioed the Coast Guard base to relay the current status of his mission.

Captain Aberdeen walked over to his XO.

He inquired, "Who's on the fifty?"

The second officer looked toward the stern. "Caine and Alexis," he replied.

In addition to the Mk 38 MGS, the Victoria was equipped with an M2 Browning .50 calibre heavy machine gun on the bridge deck just aft of the pilothouse. This gave the patrol boat the ability to defend itself against attack from any direction. The fifty cal. had a maximum range of almost seven thousand metres but its effective firing range was just under two kilometres. With a firing rate of about five hundred rounds per minute, small boats had little chance of survival unless the sailors manning the gun were merciful. The two crewmen at the M2 were wearing dark blue helmets over the protective gear that covered their head and face.

"What kinda rounds we have on the belt?" Aberdeen asked.

"Armour-piercing. Every fourth round is a tracer."

"Hmm. Like you think we at war with Trinidad?"

Both men laughed, causing some heads to turn in their direction.

*Victoria* rumbled slowly towards the blue luxury boat and twenty-five minutes later its starboard side was alongside the starboard side of the drifting craft about six hundred metres away. There was still no sign of life on board the expensive boat. The MGS was aimed at the vessel, and three sailors stood along the cutter's starboard side aiming M16 rifles at the seemingly abandoned boat.

Captain Aberdeen hailed the vessel using the external PA system. There was no response. Surely, by now someone should've heard our engines, he thought. He hailed the vessel again, this time in English and Spanish. There was no way anyone from the outside could see through the tinted glass windows of the luxury boat. So they didn't know if anyone was looking at them. The captain had now positively identified it as a Hatteras 60.

St. Paul said, "Sir, I recommend we send a boarding party to check it out."

Aberdeen agreed and ordered his Second Officer to take four

men to see what was taking place on that boat. Could pirates have raided it? It looked like it was almost new.

"Be careful," he implored his XO. "Make sure everyone is fully armed. And take a sixty with you."

A few minutes later, St. Paul and four sailors were aboard the rigid inflatable boat in the slipway in the aft of *Victoria* being lowered into the agitated waters of the Atlantic Ocean. Four of the men carried M16 rifles while the fifth sailor laid at the bow aiming an M60 machine gun ahead of them. The remaining men on the Coast Guard cutter watched tensely as the RIB skipped across the sea surface, its inboard diesel engine pushing it at twenty knots.

"Weps, make sure you keep that yacht in your sights," Aberdeen said to the Weapons Control Officer. "Single shot selection."

"Single shot selection. Aye, Sir!" repeated the young sailor, Constable Lewis. He had graduated from the T.A. Marryshow Community College, Grenada's own premier tertiary level institution, only four years ago, with an Associate's degree in IT. He chuckled as he recalled when he used to doubt his Communication Studies lecturer when the latter would tell him that he would one day be a member of the RGPF. Now here he was serving his country aboard Grenada's flagship.

Sergeant Aberdeen turned to Inspector Andrews and handed him a camcorder.

"Make yourself useful and record this operation."

Andrews may outrank Aberdeen in the RGPF, but on the sea Aberdeen was in charge. He was the captain of the boat! Andrews accepted the task silently and started recording the shrinking image of the RIB.

Suddenly the coxswain shouted, "Movement, upper deck!"

Aberdeen jammed his binoculars to his eyes and was surprised to see a man looking across at them from the fly bridge of the Hatteras and pointing somewhat frantically. Another male promptly joined him and Captain Aberdeen could see that they were trying to start the boat. He keyed the external PA system.

"THIS IS THE GRENADA COAST GUARD. STAY WHERE YOU ARE AND PREPARE TO BE BOARDED."

He repeated the command in Spanish then commanded Patrice to take *Victoria* closer. The Caterpillar engines growled loudly as the coxswain brought the patrol boat within three hundred metres of the yacht. As they drew closer, Andrews was able to pick out the name painted in small yellow letters on the bow.

"*El Tiburón*," he blurted out.

"What?" a confused Aberdeen said.

"I see the name by the bow. *El Tiburón*."

Aberdeen aimed his glasses at the bow and confirmed the name of the luxury boat.

One of the heads on the upper deck of *El Tiburón* disappeared while the other man stood looking at the RIB as it pulled alongside the hull of the blue boat. While one Grenadian sailor covered the upper deck with his rifle, St. Paul and another sailor climbed on board. The RIB began to move away from the yacht as soon as the two Coast Guardsmen were on board. As it was backing off, the individual on the fly bridge who had disappeared earlier, suddenly popped up and aimed a weapon over the side at the RIB.

"Gun!" shouted the Weapons Control Officer on *Victoria*. But he couldn't fire on *El Tiburón* without endangering his crewmates over there.

Automatic gunfire erupted as the three sailors lined up along the *Victoria*'s starboard side unleashed a volley at the man threatening their colleagues. The upper body of the would-be ambusher was riddled with dozens of 5.56 mm NATO rounds and his lifeless body along with the rifle he was holding toppled overboard into the choppy Atlantic in a big splash. The two Grenadian officers who had stormed the boat looked up in surprise. Then St. Paul led his partner aft towards the entrance to the cabin at a crouch, his M16 at shoulder level pointing the way. He was surprised to be confronted by another man who was aiming a pistol at them. St. Paul promptly let loose a three-round burst into the man's chest, but not before the man had pulled the trigger of his weapon. As the man fell dead to the deck, St. Paul also heard a thud behind him. He spun around to see his partner on the deck gasping for breath.

"I good," Noel reassured his commanding officer. "It didn't go through the vest."

St.Paul helped Noel to his feet then headed to the upper deck. Thank God for body armour! Noel shouldered his M16, unsheathed his pistol and headed into the cabin.

On *Victoria*, Inspector Andrews zoomed in on the stern of the luxury boat to get a good shot of the men entering the cabin of *El Tiburón*. He panned the camera upwards to see what the other occupant of the boat was doing. He almost dropped the camcorder when he saw the man pointing a long cylinder at the patrol boat. He recognised the weapon immediately, having seen it in propaganda videos put out by jihadist terrorists in Iraq and Afghanistan.

"RPG!" he shouted.

Every man in the air-conditioned pilothouse of *Victoria* started to sweat. Aberdeen, who had been looking at the action at the stern of *El Tiburón*, whipped his binoculars' sights up to the top of the motor yacht and his heart almost stopped.

He yelled, "Full reverse! Weps, take out that bridge!" He hoped his men hadn't yet made it up to the controls of that boat. He grabbed the radio to call base to report that his boat was under attack.

The engines of *Victoria* roared to life and the propellers churned up the water astern as the cutter started backing up desperately. A shrill alarm reverberated throughout the boat warning everyone to prepare for collision. Inspector Andrews saw a flash on *El Tiburón* as a rocket propelled grenade hurtled toward the flagship of the Grenada Coast Guard Unit.

# CHAPTER 19

The Executive Officer of *Victoria* peered up the stairway leading from the main deck to the fly bridge of *El Tiburón* and saw a Hispanic-looking man leaning over the starboard side looking towards the Grenadian Coast Guard cutter. He noticed that the man was holding a cylindrical object that could be a rocket launcher. St. Paul had a split second to make up his mind. But he wasn't taking any chances. He would answer any questions later if he was wrong. He aimed at the man's upper body and began to squeeze the trigger. At the last moment he redirected his aim and fired three rounds. The man fell backwards screaming, his fibula and tibia shattered in many places. His loud screams could not mask the whoosh then subsequent hissing that was rapidly fading in the distance. The XO quickly climbed up the steps to the bridge, and standing in a pool of fresh blood, looked across the water towards his boat, his heart in his throat. He was horrified to see a rocket-propelled grenade streaking toward a retreating *Victoria.* Was Grenada about to lose eight men and a six million-dollar patrol boat today? After about two hundred metres, the grenade lost altitude and fell harmlessly into the sea. St. Paul exhaled in relief then turned his attention to the wounded man still screaming and writhing in agony at his feet.

The XO pulled out a first aid kit from his backpack and began attending to the wounded man. As he was applying tourniquets to the man's legs, an outboard engine came to life on the port side of the motor yacht. He heard shouts followed by the unmistakable sound of the M60 in the RIB. The outboard sputtered then died.

He shouted, "Noel, what going on?"

Noel called up from the main deck a couple minutes later, "Main and lower decks clear. Dem fellas just stop a speed boat from getting away. Port side."

"Ok. Come up here and take care of this prisoner."

Noel was one of two medics stationed on *Victoria.*

St. Paul radioed *Victoria* to report the status of his mission as he walked through the main cabin. He also got a status update from his captain.

"Boy, all-you almost get it over there, you know," Aberdeen stated. "We were just about to take out the bridge and that grenade launcher when we realise you neutralise the man."

St. Paul said, "But he fired the grenade before I shot him."

"Yes, but Inspector Andrews realised *Victoria* was out of range already. You figure out who those people are?"

"They look South American to me. I searching the cabin now. I got a Venezuelan and a Colombian flag. And some huge bales of stuff downstairs. I can't even move them by me-self."

"Make sure you have a video record of everything over there. Any ID on those men?"

"None at all."

Noel shouted down to St. Paul that the prisoner was bandaged but he needed to get him to *Victoria* right away.

Meanwhile, the men in the RIB had disabled a speedboat that was trying to escape the maritime lawmen. The red and green cigarette was low in the water with cargo that was wrapped in blue plastic. Two men were arguing with each other animatedly until one dove overboard and started swimming back towards the mainland. Kamal Vincent, who was at the controls of the RIB, called *Victoria* to report. He watched the swimmer, and he and his crewmates started laughing. The remaining man in the cigarette glared at them angrily.

Vincent spoke to his captain, "Kyap, we have a Grenadian in a cigarette with some suspicious cargo. Another man trying to swim back to shore."

"Good work, Sailor," Aberdeen replied. "What's the status of the cigarette?"

"We had to disable the engine, Sir. They was trying to get away."

"Roger. Don't let that cargo sink."

"Aye, Sir."

Aberdeen had some decisions to make. He had a wounded prisoner, a foreigner. He also had two Grenadian prisoners, one of whom thought he could swim all the way back to the mainland. The sergeant thought about letting Vincent follow him all the way to land to see where he would lead them. But they didn't have time for that. Then there were the two dead bodies of non-nationals. He had a long report to write tonight. He picked up the radio to contact his Executive Officer.

"XO, can you take that boat back to base?"

The glee in St. Paul's voice couldn't be concealed as he responded in the affirmative.

*Victoria* swung around to the port side of *El Tiburón* so that Aberdeen could evaluate the scene that had been hidden from his view earlier. He whistled loudly when he saw the huge bale of cargo in the red and green speedboat.

"Inspeck, if that is coke, we make a big catch today," he said to Andrews.

The anti-narcotics officer was smiling broadly. This could be the biggest drug bust in Grenada's history. They didn't know where that yacht came from but they were able to get a prisoner. Prisoners, in fact.

"Jerry, boy, we making great progress in this war. This is a huge setback for dem drugmen and dem."

They watched as crewmen brought the Grenadian boatman and his cargo on board *Victoria.* Then the coxswain moved the cutter closer to the yacht so that they could carefully do a starboard-to-port brace with *El Tiburón* in order to transfer the wounded South American man on board. Sailors immediately brought him to sickbay and a medic tried to stabilize him. Inspector Andrews was disappointed that the foreigner was unable to speak at the moment.

Two more sailors joined St. Paul and Noel to take *El Tiburón* back to the Coast Guard base in True Blue. The men in the RIB fished the body of first attacker from the water then headed to the mother ship to be winched back into its slipway.

"Captain, what about the swimmer?" the coxswain asked.

"We'll get him on the way."

They put the two bodies in black body-bags and laid them on the main deck. More casualties in the war on White Spice. Inspector Andrews went aboard the motor yacht and was blown away by the lavish furnishing of the cabin. He could hardly believe that this cabin cost more than his house. The sleeping compartment was much more luxurious than his bedroom. He went below deck to look at the engine room. It looked like it was very well kept. The passageway was taken up by giant parcels wrapped in blue plastic. He punched one with his knuckles and was surprised by how solid it was. That's a lot of stuff! He estimated close to two tonnes of stuff.

Twenty minutes later, *Victoria* was slowly leading the way southward back to base. They were traveling with the current, so the boat wasn't pitching as much as it had been doing on its northward journey. Aberdeen and several men searched the water ahead of them with binoculars looking for the superman swimmer. They found him floundering about ten minutes later, his arms flailing wildly. Apparently, he now fancied his chances better on the Coast Guard cutter than trying to challenge the Atlantic Ocean. Aberdeen ordered St. Paul to pick him up with the yacht. He imagined the circus awaiting them at the base. He had already ordered for an ambulance and the presence of a high security detail for the prisoners as well as for the cargo believed to be cocaine. This will be a very long night, he thought.

Almost three hours later, *Victoria* and *El Tiburón* were docked at the Coast Guard Base in True Blue. The facility was over-flowing with heavily armed security personnel. Commissioner Coutain, Superintendent Telesford, and Superintendent Clifford were on hand to welcome the patrol boat with its haul. They watched as the wounded prisoner was loaded into a waiting ambulance that sped off to the General Hospital in St. George's with a heavily armed police escort. Personnel from the SSU and DS-1 took charge of the Grenadian detainees while an undertaker dealt with the bodies of the foreigners. A police videographer shot footage of some DS-1 agents unloading and cataloguing the bales of suspected drugs. They would be tested in the morning to confirm if the material was indeed cocaine. It took the anti-narcotics agents almost an hour to unload all the cargo found on the motor yacht. The commissioner and the two superintendents then met with Andrews, Aberdeen and St. Paul for a debriefing.

# CHAPTER 20

**Friday June 28**
**4:45 p.m.**
**Grenville, St. Andrew's**

The black Nissan X-Trail drove slowly through Ben Jones Street, soca music pouring through the open front windows. The heavy bass emitting from the 1200 Watt dual 12-inch MTX Terminator subwoofers caused pedestrians to turn their heads as calypsonian Shortpree's tune, *Summertime*, played on the stereo system. Some people stopped to admire the black SUV with gold spinning rims as it passed them. Junior was at the wheel while Kellon was lounging in the front passenger seat. They had to pass through Grenville on this Friday evening to pick up Junior's girlfriend just outside of this town. She was going to spend the weekend with him in Sauteurs.

"Man, Shortpree really getting better every year," Kellon remarked.

"Correct is right!" Junior said. "Is only a matter of time before he win the calypso monarch. I mean, he took the groovy crown in 2012 already."

"That is one Kayak I could say that really focus on his music," Kellon observed, referring to the fact that Shortpree was from the sister island of Carriacou.

"You sure right."

They were approaching a group of vendors selling roast corn, nuts, and drinks on the sidewalk. Junior's mouth salivated for corn.

"What the . . .!" Kellon suddenly exclaimed.

"Wha' happen?" Junior asked in surprise.

"Watch that fella over there with the white sneakers."

Junior's gaze shifted to his left to fall on a youngster about twenty-two years old, wearing white sneakers, three-quarter black jeans, and a black Chicago Bulls basketball vest over a white t-shirt. He was modelling a neat high-top box-cut fade as his hairstyle. Each finger on both hands had at least one gold ring on it. He was also sporting more than a few gold chains around his neck. The cousins laughed.

"What year is this, Cuz?" Kellon asked Junior.

Junior laughed, recognizing where this was going.

"Must be 1993," he replied sarcastically.

They both laughed then Kellon suddenly stopped laughing and grabbed his cousin's left hand which was on the gearstick.

"Pull up there a minute," he instructed Junior. "Not drugs I just see he selling dey?"

"What!" Junior exclaimed incredulously. He pulled over to the sidewalk in front of a bar. A group of middle-aged men was sitting outside drinking beers and slamming dominoes.

Kellon leaned out of his window and beckoned to the Mr. T wannabe. The young man came over uncertainly.

"What you want?" he asked gruffly. Sunlight glinted off a couple of gold-capped incisors.

"What you have?" Kellon enquired as he looked up at the five-foot-nine inch youth.

The young man responded that he had some White Spice.

"What?" Kellon asked, puzzled.

"Man, is coke," hissed the youth impatiently. "You want?"

Kellon exchanged a glance with his cousin then turned back to the drug dealer.

"Man, you better get outta here with that stuff."

"What!" the youth didn't take that directive lightly. "You know who you dealing with? You better move along before you get hurt."

He steupsed and turned to walk off. Kellon's left hand suddenly shot out of the window and grabbed him by the neck, pulling him back.

"*You* know who you dealing with?" Kellon snarled. His right hand came up with his Glock and he pressed it against the drug dealer's left temple.

The youngster's eyes opened wide and tears started streaming down his face as he quaked in Kellon's hand.

"Lemme see some ID," Kellon ordered. "Pull out your wallet slowly and toss it to the driver here."

The smell of urine drifted to the inside of the X-Trail. Kellon sniffed the air as a dog would, and snickered.

"Man, you go and make the boy pee himself," Junior laughed. Then he suddenly remembered his own experience a few months ago and stopped laughing.

The youth tossed his wallet to Junior who checked it for an ID.

"His name is Antonio Johnson, from Woburn," he reported.

Kellon looked at Antonio for a few seconds before speaking.

"Look here, don't be selling your crap here in Grenville. If I ever see you again, you might lose your head. You ketch me?"

Antonio was shaking uncontrollably and sobbing, attracting the attention of the men in front of the bar, and other street vendors. The domino players had stopped their game to check out what was going on at the stationary Nissan. A big-bottom female vendor shouted to the vehicle.

"Yes! Manners him! He only selling he dirty drugs here. And dem police not doing nothing. Time for somebody to do something about dem men and dem."

"You hear me?" Kellon yelled again at Antonio. "Take that crap somewhere else."

Kellon was loud enough for people on the sidewalk to hear him.

"Boy, let's go," Junior said to him. "This attracting too much attention now."

Junior handed Antonio's wallet back to him. The youth's nostrils were leaking as if he had suddenly gotten the flu.

"Ye-ye-yes, Sir," Antonio stuttered to Kellon. "You won't see me here again."

"I better not," Kellon warned him.

He shoved Antonio backwards causing him to fall on his butt on the dirty sidewalk. The curious crowd laughed at the drug dealer who only minutes ago was the don on the block.

Junior glanced in his rearview mirror to see two uniformed police officers approaching. He pulled out into the street to continue the journey to St. Patrick's. He had to make a stop in Paradise to pick up Vernelle first. He laughed as they drove slowly but hurriedly up the rest of Ben Jones Street, heads bobbing to a beat by the Haitian group Harmonik.

"I can't believe you just did that," he said to Kellon. "Not you who run away scared from Levera beach a few months ago?"

Kellon smiled and shook his head.

"So you giving me talk now!" he said, punching his cousin's left shoulder playfully.

"You realise who that fella most likely is?" Junior said seriously.

"You think he is one of those Johnson people from Woburn?"

"It can't be a coincidence. A Johnson from Woburn selling coke?"

They knew that that Johnson family was dabbling in the drug business but they didn't realise they were into selling stuff on the street.

Junior voiced what they were both thinking.

"If he is one of them, you know they will retaliate."

"Damn!" Kellon exclaimed softly as he pounded his fist on the dashboard. "But I just don't like seeing people sell drugs to our people."

Junior took his eyes off the pot-holed road for a few seconds to look across at his cousin, wondering if he realised the irony in that statement.

"Yeah, I know, I know," Kellon said grinning. "But whoever we sending the stuff to in the States certainly not selling it to Grenadians."

Junior grunted in agreement.

They continued the journey in silence, taking in the music from the stereo system. But they were both thinking about if and how the Johnsons would retaliate. They stopped for Vernelle in the village of Paradise then sped on to Sauteurs.

# CHAPTER 21

**Sunday September 29**
**2:37 p.m.**
**Progress Park, St. Andrew's**

Kellon and Junior were among the scores of people gathered at Progress Park on this sunny afternoon to enjoy the twenty-twenty cricket match. The village of Hermitage in St. Patrick's was taking on a team of policemen from the Grenville police station. This was a fete-match, part of the community policing effort of the RGPF. The Grenville officers had lost the first match played in Hermitage the previous Sunday, by only two runs. Now they were hoping to even the series in this highly anticipated clash. Music blared from huge speaker boxes as a DJ played a selection of local soca. Children were running around kicking footballs on the edge of the field, or cheerfully eating cotton candy and snow cones. The mouth-watering aroma of spicy BBQ chicken and the sweet scent of roasting corn floated over the spectators' positions.

The Alexanders, including Jeffery, were there to support the Hermitage team. Junior had found a great parking spot along the main road outside the fence that surrounded the field, and the three fellas were leaning or sitting on the X-Trail. They were all drinking beers, and Jeffery was halfway through a chicken roti. Junior and Kellon looked at him in astonishment, mouths half-open, because they knew that he had just finished eating a chicken sandwich.

"Boy, you kyan' done eat?" Junior said to Jeffery.

Jeffrey grinned at him then went off to get a bowl of lambie waters, finishing the roti on the way. He returned less than three minutes later with a Styrofoam bowl steaming with the broth.

"All-you ain't realise something?" he asked Junior and Kellon.

They turned to him expectantly, awaiting an answer.

"Well all-you really does notice you surroundings," the teenager said sarcastically. "Look on both sides of us. Only black SUV's."

Junior and Kellon gazed to their right then to the left and were surprised to see that theirs was one of seven black SUV's parked side-by-side facing the field. They looked at each other with puzzled expressions. What a coincidence!

"I guess birds of similar plumage congregate," Junior remarked.

"Wha'?" Jeffrey asked, puzzled.

"Birds of one feather flock together," Junior explained impatiently. "Man, all-you don't do proverbs in school again?"

To their left was a black Kia Sportage. Parked on the right of their X-Trail were a shiny black BMW X3, two 2012 Hyundai Tucsons, a Jeep Grand Cherokee belonging to the RGPF, and a mud-covered Range Rover.

"Man, you realise that most of those SUV's nowadays are driven by women?" Jeffrey observed.

"That's right, bwoy," Kellon replied. "So you better recognise they won't need to ask you for a ride when you get yours."

The lawmen were about to start their inning. They had to make ninety-six runs to win the match. As the opening batsmen took their places at the crease to begin the chase, cheers went up from the crowd. There seemed to be an unusually large number of young females taking in this match. Kellon smiled and shook his head in disbelief because he knew young ladies don't usually go to cricket matches. Police officers from other stations around the country were also present to support their colleagues. They were all dressed in civilian attire but they were still recognisable as officers. Some hung out inside the fence, while others gathered around mobile bars on the outside, old-talking, drinking beers and throwing back shots of rum.

Shouts and cheers went up from the crowd everytime the batsmen hit a boundary. After the first over, the lawmen had already raced to nineteen without loss.

"Wait, not Boyo who batting?" Junior groaned.

Boyo Cyrus was an opening batsman for Grenada and the Windward Islands. The twenty-four-year old was a prolific scorer and could almost single-handedly turn a match around. He was a corporal in the RGPF, and his presence at today's match spelt doom for the Hermitage team even before a single ball had been bowled.

"Well you know Hermitage lose already," Kellon conceded, shaking his head sorrowfully.

"Fellas, watch that over there," Jeffrey interrupted their lamentation between sips of his lambie waters.

They all looked at three young ladies in very short tight skirts struggling to walk as they approached the line of parked SUV's. The policemen drinking on the other side of the road stopped their conversations and also stared at the girls. One inspector frowned as the girls' skirts barely covered their behinds. He couldn't believe that parents allowed their daughters to go out dressed like that.

"Well, I know dem girls kyant siddown," Junior joked.

Kellon and Jeffrey snickered.

"You think they 'fraid?" Kellon replied. "Doh make joke!"

Suddenly there was a crack as Boyo Cyrus hit the ball hard and high back over the head of the very frustrated bowler. The batsman joined everyone in admiring the white ball as it soared over the vehicles parked outside the fence, over the road, over the vehicles parked on the other side of the road, towards the Paradise River.

As the cricket ball sails over the fence, a red beat-up four-door Suzuki Vitara crawls slowly down the straight stretch of road towards Progress Park. Nobody pays attention to the rusting vehicle as its occupants seem to search for a parking spot. Almost every head is turned upward to admire the flight of the ball. Hardly anyone notices two bodies leaning out of the right-side windows brandishing mini-UZI machine pistols. The police officers drinking on the river side of the road are all staring up at the ball coming towards them when a few notices two bodies sticking out of the right side windows of the jalopy.

"Well what kinda stunt is that now?" Inspector Jones of the Grenville Police Station exclaims as he observes the approaching Suzuki. "And he doh even have license plate!"

As the officers are on the opposite side of the road, they cannot see that both figures have masks over their faces,. It is a left-hand drive vehicle, the driver being on the same side as the socialising policemen.

ASP Rudolph is about to chime in with his own comment when the loud staccato of automatic gunfire punctuates the bassline of the soca music blasting from the massive speakers on the other side of the field.

"Take cover!" Jones shouts. "Drive-by!"

All the policemen on the left side of the road dive to the ground, and crawl behind vehicles to take cover. Only three are armed with pistols. They hear bullets tear into metal, and people scream in terror and pain. It takes the Vitara three long seconds to pass the parked SUV's, and within that time the masked gunmen empty their 25-round magazines, spraying in figure eight patterns. One woman runs towards her Kia Sportage trying to protect her baby, and is cut down in a hail of bullets. The Alexander boys heave to the ground in front of their X-Trail, cowering, hearing the tyres on the Nissan hiss as slugs penetrate them causing air to escape. The vehicle drops a few inches lower to the ground. Junior trembles in terror and rage as his beloved ride appears to be disintegrating before his very eyes. Glass is flying everywhere as windows and windshields shatter. A stray bullet flies between the BMW X3 and a Hyundai Tucson, whizzes by the right ear of the umpire and slams into Boyo's left shoulder, shattering it along with his dreams of playing professional cricket in the future. The unlucky corporal crumbles to the ground screaming in agony.

Kellon dared to look around a front tyre of their Nissan and was horrified to see Toni Diaz dragging herself towards them shrieking loudly. His eyes opened wide as he realised that her legs were angled oddly behind her as she crawled toward them. He shouted in anguish and stood up to run to his Latin lover. Junior's hand shot up and pulled him back down but he threw off his cousin and scrambled on hands and knees towards his woman.

"Toni!" he bawled, cradling her head in his lap.

Around him people were also screaming and crying, but he could only hear Toni's cries. The music had finally stopped. Everyone forgot about the match. Bloodied bodies were everywhere. Some dead, some wounded. Men, women, and children. Civilians and police officers. By then, the attackers had disappeared around the corner, crossing the Paradise bridge to the other side of St. Andrew's. A dozen vehicles, including the row of seven black SUV's, were badly shot up while six people were killed on the spot by the hail of bullets. More than twenty-five people were wounded including nine police officers.

Inspector Jones dialled headquarters on his cellphone to request backup. He then called the SSU base at the old Pearls Airport less than five minutes away so that they could begin the search for the bandits. Who were those gunmen? He couldn't imagine who would be so crazy to attack the police. The officers who weren't wounded began helping the victims of the attack.

Vehicles raced towards Princess Alice hospital in Mirabeau with the wounded. Some cars headed towards The General Hospital in St. George's, knowing that it made no sense going to the under-equipped rural hospital with the critically wounded. Two of those critically wounded who were heading to the capital never made it alive. Never in the history of Grenada had such violence been witnessed during peacetime. Inspector Jones looked at the mayhem, clenched his jaw and swore to avenge the attack on his officers. He turned to regard the approaching Superintendent Lennox Bradford, the officer in charge of the Eastern Division, who was on his cellphone in an intense conversation with the commissioner. Bradford finished his call, consulted with Jones, and both men walked over to check out the crime scene. Two ambulances arrived with sirens blaring along with the first detectives from the Grenville Police Station. Half an hour later, four more detectives arrived from St. George's. Commissioner Coutain pulled up in her black Prado, noting with satisfaction a dozen heavily-armed personnel of the SSU trying to secure the area. The commissioner called the Prime Minister to describe the afternoon's events, nodding in approval as she saw Inspector Jones using his cellphone to record the entire scene on video. She groaned inwardly as she took in the carnage, already plotting a response to this heinous crime against whoever the guilty parties were. It would be a very grim press conference on Monday.

# CHAPTER 22

Antonio Johnson looked through the back window of the Suzuki at the chaos that was taking place at Progress Park after they had sprayed the Alexanders and their precious vehicle with bullets. As they rounded the corner to cross the Paradise bridge, he grinned in satisfaction, knowing that he had put a hurting on those fools. It was the first time in three months that his brothers, who were with him in the Vitara, had seen him smile.

After he had been thoroughly humiliated in Grenville by Kellon and Junior Alexander three months ago, Antonio had sprinted through the streets of the town to the jetty to take his speedboat back to their coastal compound in Woburn. He had taken the wheel himself, his two brothers holding on for dear life as he ignored the waves of the Atlantic on the way down the east coast. He had almost swamped the fiberglass boat twice. His brothers were very grateful when they were safely berthed at their jetty in Woburn.

The Johnson boys' father was enraged when Antonio had told him about the incident in Grenville. That encounter with the Alexanders had probably cost him $5000 that evening. The senior Johnson had done some business with the Sauteurs fellas before, so he was surprised to hear what had transpired in Grenville with his son. He was already taking some heat after being suspected of supplying his nephew at MBIA with drugs to send to Miami. He had instructed Antonio not to back down the next time the Alexanders or anyone else tried to embarrass them.

For his part, Antonio was a changed man after that humiliating experience. He had vowed that he would get even with those guys. He had spent many sleepless nights trying to figure out what to do. He had considered firebombing Universal Electronics, the business owned by the Alexanders at the Frequente Industrial Park. But he didn't want to take away jobs from the innocent employees there. Besides, he sometimes bought electronics from their store. So he and his brothers, Joe and Kendall, had decided to head to Sauteurs on this Sunday afternoon to shoot up the conspicuously coloured Alexander mansion on High Street.

As they were driving through Grenville on the way to Sauteurs, Antonio had received a phone call from his cousin, Damion, telling him that Kellon and Junior were liming at a cricket game in Progress Park, *only three minutes away*. It was just the opportunity he had been looking for. He had been even more elated to learn that the pompous idiots were sitting outside the field on their vehicle. The Johnson brothers had taken the decision to do the drive-by shooting at Progress Park instead of at Sauteurs. They would have to abandon the vehicle somewhere but it was an old one anyway. They had stopped about a half mile before Progress Park to hurriedly remove the license plates. Their mini-UZIs locked and loaded, they had raced to the Park searching for the black SUV in the spot where their cousin had said it would be. They were shocked to find several black SUV's parked together. The brothers had then decided to shoot up all of them and figure it out later.

Joe, who was driving, shouted to Antonio for instructions. He needed to know which road to take at the round-about after the bridge. They could turn right and head to Pearls Airport, or turn left towards Dunfermline.

"Head for Pearls!" Antonio instructed.

"Boy, you crazy?" Kendall shouted, alarm in his voice. "We heading right for dem SSU."

"Joe, just drive," Antonio tried to sound calm. He was panting at this point. He reached for a bottle of Glenelg spring water and gulped down the entire half-litre. He belched loudly with satisfaction.

The Johnson brothers sped through the village of Simon, raced by the SSU camp at Pearls Airport, and turned the corner at the far end of the road just as two pickups filled with armed paramilitary personnel peeled out of the base to head to Progress Park. The three brothers began looking for a suitable place to abandon the vehicle. Antonio was on his phone giving his cousin directions on where to meet them. Joe turned into a dirt road in Upper Pearls and found a clump of trees where they could abandon and destroy the jalopy.

Fred Joseph, a 58-year old farmer, was weeding his garden at Upper Pearls when the relative quietness of the Sunday afternoon was shattered by the din of a very old vehicle. He looked up in annoyance to be greeted by the sight of a dirty red "jeep" coming up the gravel road. He wondered who could be driving in here. Young lovers would never drive in such a dirty, noisy vehicle to look for a spot to make out. He remained in his stooping position as he watched attentively. He was surprised to see three young men hop out. His attention was especially drawn to the guns that two of them were carrying. He tried to crouch even lower between his rows of corn. He was glad that he was wearing dark-coloured clothes which camouflaged him in the brush. His lips curled into a thin smile as he recalled his days as a soldier in the PRA from 1981 – 1983.

Farmer Fred held his breath as the three men huddled in quiet discussion, then the one who seemed to be the leader lit a bottle of what seemed to be a Molotov cocktail and heaved it into the Suzuki. Fred had a feeling these guys were up to no good. He pulled out a Blackberry Bold, activated the video app and started shooting. The three men stood a few metres from the burning vehicle to watch it. As they walked back down the road, the Vitara exploded. Fred threw himself flat onto the ground, wishing he were a worm. After about ten minutes, a white Toyota Corolla drove up and the trio got in. Fred got a good shot of the number plate of the Corolla as it turned to head back down the dirt road. After the car disappeared around the corner, he deactivated the video app and pocketed his Blackberry. He reminded himself that he needed to call the police when he got home after he was done weeding. *I not wasting no credit to call 9-1-1 now*, he thought to himself.

# CHAPTER 23

**Monday September 30**
**8:20 a.m.**
**Sauteurs, St. Patrick's**

Junior and Kellon stared blankly at the walls behind each other as they sat at opposite sides of their seven-piece dining set, ignoring the plates of their mouth-watering West Indian breakfast that stared up at them. Although the housekeeper had dutifully prepared and served their morning meal, they didn't feel like eating. Kellon was still teary-eyed over his severely injured girlfriend. Toni had lost both legs and was in intensive care at The General Hospital in St. George's. She had lost a lot of blood. Fortunately, he and Jeffrey had the same blood type as the Cuban lady, so they each had donated a pint to aid in her recovery. But the doctors couldn't save her legs. They were badly shot up. Junior was thinking about Toni also, but he was mourning the destruction of his beloved X-Trail. He had spent over US$10,000 to pimp his Nissan. He had installed a top-of-the-line stereo system with twelve-inch titanium sub-woofers; a seven-inch touch-screen monitor for a multimedia entertainment centre for passengers riding in the back; fog lamps; mag wheels with spinning gold rims; and a few other accessories. Now his ride was shot up so badly that it was beyond repair. Nothing could be saved in or on it.

"Man, I sure is dem Johnson fellas who do that," Kellon said, his eyes boring holes in the opposite wall, and a deep scowl plastered on his face. His mood had been alternating between anger, sadness and confusion since Sunday evening when Toni had passed out as he had held her head after she had been shot.

"I want to believe you, bro," Junior said. "Once we confirm it, we going after dem."

Kellon started to pick absent-mindedly at his saltfish souse with his fork. Tears fell into his plate as he thought about how close Toni had come to dying. Now she was sentenced to a wheelchair for the rest of her life. Junior watched his cousin sadly and he started to weep as well, for Toni, but more so for his X-Trail.

"Let's wait for word from the police," Junior suggested between sobs.

Kellon nodded in agreement. They were both very tired, having spent the entire night at the hospital. Scores of people had gathered at the hospital all night as word had spread about the attack at Progress Park. Every single police officer was now on active duty. The Prime Minister came close to calling a state of emergency but Commissioner Coutain eventually convinced him that that wasn't necessary at the moment. The Grenadian leader now moved around with no less than ten heavily armed men of the elite Rapid Response Unit, in addition to his regular detail of four men from Special Branch. He also wore body armour under his shirt. Members of the regular constabulary of the RGPF were now accompanied by a pair of officers from the Special Services Unit armed with M16 rifles. Every officer on patrol now wore Kevlar body armour. Most people were very surprised that the RGPF had so much equipment.

"Yeah. My boy in Grenville will tell us if they come up with any suspects," Kellon said glumly.

The Alexander cousins tried to eat their breakfast but gave up after only a few bites. Taking their cups of cocoa, they headed to the living-room to check out the Government Information Service television news.

## Grenville Police Station
## Grenville, St. Andrew's

Commissioner Coutain scrutinised the bloodshot eyes and tired faces of three of the five men who sat with her at the table in the meeting room of the Grenville Police Station. Superintendent Bradford and Inspector Jones had been up all night coordinating the investigation of the Progress Park drive-by shooting from the Grenville Police Station. Neither man had grabbed more than thirty minutes sleep over the past twenty-four hours. ASP Sylvester, Grenada's head detective, was also at the meeting after having spent all night at the crime scene with four other detectives gathering evidence. All three men were exhausted as they were trying to solve this case expeditiously. But they had hit a blank wall. Nobody had gotten a good view of the perpetrators. Superintendents Jimmy Duncan and Levy Grant of the RRU and SSU, respectively, completed the group of six discussing the attack on the police fete-match.

"Mr. Sylvester," Commissioner Coutain turned to face the head of CID. "Do we have any idea who would so brazenly attack the police?"

The chief detective looked at the commissioner with blank eyes. He and his men hadn't gotten any fingerprints from the spent shells that littered the road outside the playing field, or from bullets dug out of bodies and vehicles.

He answered the commissioner, "No, ma'am. Not a single print on any shell casing or slug. Nobody saw the shooters. And we don't know where the vehicle is now."

"I can't believe our country is so big that we cannot find a single vehicle," Commissioner Coutain said, her British accent making it hard for the men to become annoyed at her condescending tone.

"I saw the vehicle," Inspector Jones said. "It was an old piece of Suzuki. Red. Those things are popular in this country. And this one had no license plates."

"Hmm, I see the problem," the commissioner conceded. "So didn't you see the occupants of the vehicle, Inspector?"

"No, they had bandanas over their faces. And they had on shades and caps."

"Like those fellas think of everything," Superintendent Duncan said.

"Tell us what was the damage," Coutain said.

Sylvester pulled out a sheet of paper from a manila folder and looked at the data.

"Six killed on site; two died en route to The General Hospital; three died earlier this morning from their injuries. No police officers died from this attack."

There was a collective sigh of relief in the room.

Sylvester continued, "But nine officers were wounded, including Boyo . . ."

Superintendent Grant suddenly sat upright. He almost shouted, "What! Corporal Cyrus? We top batsman?"

Sylvester nodded. They all hung their heads sadly.

"Where he got shot?" Grant asked.

Sylvester said, "In the shoulder. While he was still at the crease."

"Will he be able to play cricket again?" Commissioner Coutain asked, concerned.

"It's too early to tell," Sylvester replied. He continued reading from his list.

"So in all, twenty-six injured survivors are now at the General Hospital."

"What about their conditions?" the commissioner asked.

"I think only two are in ICU," Sylvester responded. He grabbed a bottle of water and took a long swig.

Inspector Jones used his phone to order for refreshments for the officers in the room. Most of them were very hungry. He wasn't sure if they would be able to eat in this very emotional state, but they needed to keep up their strength, for what could be a very long investigation.

Superintendent Duncan asked Sylvester, "So what about damage to property?"

"Ten vehicles sustained heavy damage. Interestingly, five of them were very badly shot up."

The commissioner's head jerked up from a document she was skimming.

"Really?" she said with raised eyebrows. "And do we know who they belong to?"

"We're working on that right now," Sylvester replied. "But one is ours, a Jeep Cherokee from Camp Salines."

Superintendent Grant groaned. That was one fewer vehicle available to the Force. He said, "Yes, Sergeants Richards and Bernard signed it out yesterday in truth. I forgot about that."

"Are Richards and Bernard okay?" Commissioner Coutain asked.

"Yes," Grant answered. "They helped out with securing the area after the attack. They came back to camp this morning."

"The interesting thing is, those five are all black," Sylvester continued with his report.

"You don't say!" Coutain sat up slowly. "Maybe that's something."

Inspector Jones suddenly slapped the table hard, his eyes opening wide.

"One of those rides is dem Alexander car," he blurted out excitedly. "The X-Trail. They were sitting on it during the match."

"You mean those Alexander blokes from Sauteurs?" Commissioner Coutain inquired. "Is that significant?"

"Yes, those blokes!" replied Jones, unconsciously mimicking the commissioner's British accent. "It might mean something."

"Find out who the owners of those black vehicles are and we might have a lead," suggested the commissioner. "We've been assuming the perps were attacking the police. Maybe there was another motive."

"So what will we do when we find out who did this?" Superintendent Duncan asked coolly. His RRU were eager to take the fight to the hoods who shot police officers. His nephew was among the wounded officers now warded at The General Hospital. The rookie was shot in the knees and would most likely never be a law enforcement officer again.

Commissioner Coutain paused for a few seconds before responding.

"Obviously, these people are well armed. So we have to organise a well-planned operation to capture them."

Duncan smiled knowingly. He knew the RRU would be called upon to deal with that threat. He looked at the top man of the SSU and saw him smiling also.

"Make no mistake, this is not to be a revenge mission," Coutain warned. "No extra-judicial executions and the like!"

"By the way, do you know what weapons were used?" she turned back to Sylvester.

The top detective looked at Superintendent Duncan as if he needed support on this one. After all, Duncan was the soldier.

"The ballistics expert said it was most likely a high-powered machine pistol, probably a Uzi."

Inspector Jones said, "Yes, those guns fired at a very high rate. How much rounds you think they used?"

"So far, we pick up forty-six spent casings."

Duncan nodded with each statement Sylvester made about the weapons. He was present when the ballistics expert, Sergeant Joanna Crawford, had examined the evidence and made her conclusion.

Just then, Sylvester's phone beeped to signal an incoming email. He opened it and smiled when he saw the content of the new message.

He said, "I got the names of the owners of those other four black vehicles: Junior Alexander, Cheryl Jackson, John Titus and Ronald Ash."

"What do we know about them? Did they survive?" Commissioner asked.

"Only Ms. Jackson got killed," Sylvester replied. "The Kia

Sportage was hers. Apparently, she was running to it to try to protect it from the bullets."

"Hmm. Maybe the attackers concentrated their fire on those cars because they had a specific target," suggested Coutain.

"I agree," Sylvester said. "Alexander is a suspected drugman. Cheryl Jackson and Ronald Ash are bankers. John Titus is a retiree who just come back from England."

"So apart from Titus, the other three most likely have enemies," Superintendent Bradford chimed in. He had been listening quietly to the discussion, his mind working on a theory. He recalled a report he had read about three months ago about an incident in Grenville.

"How you figure those bankers have enemies?" Inspector Charles asked Bradford.

"In this economy, you know how many people get turn down for loans?" Bradford replied. "People could get mad because of that."

"True but unlikely," Commissioner Coutain said. She looked at Superintendent Bradford intently. "Do you have something in mind, Mr. Bradford?"

"Inspector, you remember a few months ago we got a report about an altercation between those same Alexanders and some other fellas?" Bradford turned to the man in charge of the Grenville Police Station.

Inspector Jones nodded. There had been a rumour that one Alexander had held a gun to a drug dealer's head to chase him off the street.

"Yes," Jones said. "We couldn't believe a suspected druglord would run a drug dealer from selling his stuff on the street."

"Maybe it was a turf thing," Coutain surmised.

"Nah, those Alexander fellas don't do anything in Grenville," Bradford said. "They only pass through."

"So do you think this is revenge for that incident?" the commissioner asked thoughtfully.

Someone knocked loudly on the door and Inspector Jones invited the person to enter. It was about time they got their sandwiches and juice. He was surprised to see a corporal standing in the doorway, not with food in hand, but with a Blackberry cellphone.

"What is it, Corporal?" Jones asked impatiently.

"Sir, you will want to see this," the corporal responded, thrusting the phone towards his commanding officer.

"What is that?" Jones inquired suspiciously.

"Sir, a man bring in video he take with his phone that could help find the suspects of the attack."

Inspector Jones almost snatched the phone from the corporal's hand.

"Who is the man? You know him?"

"His name is Fred Joseph. From Pearls."

Jones played the video on the phone and the other officers looked at him curiously as his eyes widened progressively with each passing minute.

He called out to the chief detective.

"Mr. Sylvester, lemme put this video on your laptop."

In less than three minutes, the video clip was uploaded onto Sylvester's laptop and Inspector Jones deleted it from the Blackberry.

"Make sure you get all contact information from Mr. Joseph," he ordered the corporal as he returned the cellphone. "And don't tell anyone what you saw on that clip."

After the corporal left, the officers crowded around Sylvester's laptop to check out the video clip. Audible gasps escaped from several lungs as they recognised what they had.

"That's the van that did the drive-by!" Inspector Jones announced, jabbing an index finger at the screen.

Everyone in the room believed him.

"Anybody knows who Fred Joseph is?" Commissioner Coutain asked. "Will he be a credible witness?"

"We were in the army together," Duncan replied. "During the Revolution."

Only the commissioner and Superintendent Grant knew that Duncan was a soldier in the People's Revolutionary Army in the early 1980's. The other officers turned to look at the former PRA soldier with a greater degree of respect.

"So yes," Duncan continued. "Fred will make a good witness."

"All we have to do is find the owner of that car and we have our attackers," Detective Superintendent Sylvester declared. "Fred got us a good shot of the license plate."

They all looked at the clip again.

Sylvester then logged into the RGPF Traffic Database and entered the license plate number of the white Corolla that had picked up the bandits. He whistled in surprise when he saw the corresponding data.

"Well, well, well," he said. "The Johnson name just keep coming up."

The CID man relayed the data to the others in the room. Twenty minutes later, he, Grant, Duncan, and two other detectives were heading to the site of the burnt out Suzuki in Upper Pearls to gather evidence and talk to Fred Joseph.

**High Street**
**Sauteurs, St. Patrick's**

Kellon's phone alerted him that a text message had arrived. He accessed his Whatsapp and bolted upright on the couch. He showed the message to Junior. *The police had a lead on the Progress Park attackers*! Kellon smiled slightly as he thought of what he would do to the people who were responsible for crippling Toni. Junior grinned evilly as he imagined himself pounding to a pulp the people who had shot up his beloved X-Trail. All they had to do was wait on the police to officially confirm the identity of the perpetrators. Then they would lead a posse from Sauteurs to take care of those cowards in Woburn.

# CHAPTER 24

**Monday September 30**
**2:35 p.m.**
**Maurice Bishop International Airport**

Agents Nathaniel Jacob, Salisha Charles and Robert Sam chatted outside the departure terminal building of the MBIA, observing people as they unloaded suitcases and other pieces of luggage from taxis, vans, pick-ups, cars and buses. They were amused at how these people seemed so anxious as they fussed over the simplest of things in preparation for the trans-Atlantic flight to London, England. Their observation was more than casual as they sought to identify possible drug traffickers in the ongoing war on White Spice. The operation had been going on for months, and DS-1 had caught sixteen drug mules who were foolish enough to try to get their contraband past the various levels of security at the airport. Inspector Andrews and his team were dumbfounded that even in this period of heightened alertness, people would still attempt to engage in drug trafficking. But these were the small fries; they really needed to catch the big fish.

The DS-1 agents were all dressed in civilian attire. Sergeant Charles was dressed modestly in a green shirt that hung over blue jeans. Her outfit was completed by a pair of white Keds Champion sneakers. Her black handbag with her handgun, police ID, and an extra clip of ammo was slung over her right shoulder. Her shoulder-length hair was tied back with a scrunchy to keep stray strands out of her eyes. A pair of ladies sunglasses shielded her eyes from the afternoon glare. She looked at Sergeant Jacob and raised an eyebrow.

"Natto, why you doh dress better dan dat?" she snapped at her partner. "Turn you kyap around and look like a good boy!"

Jacob let out a steupse, sucking in air between pursed lips and clenched teeth as only a West Indian could. His XXL Green Bay Packers jersey concealed a pistol secured in a holster strapped to his lower back. A blue New York Yankees baseball cap was perched high on his head with the bill facing backwards.

"You too stupid, gyul," he retorted. "Like you forget we undercover?"

All three officers laughed. The airport security personnel and most other employees at the airport knew they were anti-narcotic agents. They usually patrolled the departure and arrival lounges to check out suspicious passengers. Sometimes, they stood in line with arriving passengers to listen to conversations. At other times, they did walk-throughs with their K-9 partners. The black Labs were highly trained dogs that could sniff out drugs hidden deep within luggage or on various parts of a person's body. They had already passed through the arrival lounge, scoping out passengers and asking a few questions to some who looked too nervous as they awaited attendance by an immigration officer. They had been particularly interested in a fat-looking woman who seemed to be getting more nervous as she got closer to the immigration booth. They had intercepted her after she had cleared immigration to inquire why she seemed to be so nervous. They soon learnt that she was six months pregnant and was going through a bout of sickness. The airport nurse on duty was called to attend to her.

"Ah coming back, I going and pass some water," Corporal Sam said with a sense of urgency in his voice.

The two sergeants looked at him in surprise.

"You have bladder problems?" Charles asked. "I find you going and pee often."

Sam ignored them and jogged off to find the nearest washroom.

Charles and Jacob turned their attention to the people and traffic outside the check-in area. Airport Security personnel seemed to be doing a decent job regulating the flow of traffic. No vehicle was allowed to remain stationary for more than five minutes. People were to drop off departing passengers and their luggage within that timeframe. A lady exited the terminal building only to see her Range Rover being towed away. She took off sprinting, screaming and cursing after the tow truck, much to the amusement of the agents and other onlookers.

"Wait, that is not the former senator?" Jacob asked, as he looked at the receding figure of the short, fair lady.

"She self," Charles replied. "That lady could run fast, *oui*."

"Doh worry, she getting she van back real quick," Jacob said with confidence. "You know she paying that $100 on the spot."

"Boy, who tell you she paying anything?" Charles rebutted. "She making a few calls and getting she ride back without coughing up a cent."

The two officers returned their attention to the line of vehicles that continued to pull up in front of the departure terminal. A yellow "old school" Toyota minibus pulled up and no less than thirty-six children filed out of the vehicle that was meant to hold seventeen passengers.

"Traffic Department really slacking," Sergeant Charles remarked as she observed the obvious traffic violation.

A black Suzuki Grand Vitara pulled up, blasting a rap rhythm whose bass line rattled the glass doors of the terminal building and caused people's internal organs to vibrate. The profane language that emanated from the rap single caused some middle-aged and senior people to pause momentarily and stare disapprovingly at the source of the annoying song. An airport security officer approached the driver of the vehicle to ask him to turn down the music. The driver exited his vehicle after turning off the engine but left the music on at the same level. The tall, muscular man looked down scornfully at the security officer then headed to the other side of his ride to open the front door for his passenger. He then went to the back to unload three suitcases.

"Check that out," Sergeant Charles nodded towards the Vitara.

Jacob took in the scene and was tempted to walk up to the vehicle to identify himself as a police officer and order the driver to turn off the music. But they were under orders to remain incognito for as long as possible. His blood was beginning to boil in anger. He hated loud music. He clenched and unclenched his fists a couple of times and took a few deep breaths.

"Take it easy, man," Charles tried to calm him. She looked around and was relieved to see a uniformed constable along with a an SSU officer dressed in camouflaged BDU approach the Vitara.

The two uniformed officers spoke to the ill-mannered man and he reluctantly turned off his music. *Nobody argues with an officer of the Special Services Unit!* His passenger, a thick woman in her early twenties, stepped out of the vehicle and began pulling one of the suitcases into the terminal. Sergeant Charles could not help laughing as she took in the young lady's outfit. The relatively short lady stood in and on a pair of black platform pumps. The elevated shoes made her appear to be about five feet ten inches tall. A pair of purple high-waist skinny-legs stretchy pants disclosed every curve on her lower body from hips to ankles. A yellow plus-size strappy swing vest top struggled to cover her breasts and abdomen.

"Why women does make demselves see so much trouble?" Sergeant Charles asked rhetorically. "I wonder how long it took for her to put on those pants?"

The comically dressed young lady made Jacob forget how angry he was. His crooked teeth flashed as he broke into a grin.

"That is a lot of load she carrying around on her feet," Jacob surmised. "Imagine she ha' to wear that for eight hours on that flight!"

"All in the name of fashion," Charles scoffed.

The young woman returned to collect her second suitcase while

Charles and Jacob resumed observing other people who were scurrying around. A high-pitched scream sliced through the roar of the plane engine of an aircraft that lifted off the runway on the other side of the terminal building. The officers whirled around in the direction of the lady they were just laughing at. She was on her hands and knees on the sidewalk in front of the automatic sliding doors that led to the interior of the building. Apparently, she had not lifted her trailing foot high enough to clear the sidewalk as she stepped up from the pavement. Tears caused streaks to appear on the makeup that caked her face. The officers ran up to help her.

"Miss, you okay?" Sergeant Charles asked with great concern.

Sergeant Jacob reached down to help her up. He looked at her muscular companion who simply stood frozen, looking down at the woman strangely. As she turned to sit on the sidewalk, she lifted her knees to brush off some dirt. Jacob's eyes were focused on her right shoe whose platform was now broken. Small, white balls appeared to be inside a hollow cavity.

"Hold Tallboy dey!" he shouted to his partner, pointing to the tall muscleman while never taking his eyes off the woman.

The tall man didn't wait for the order to be obeyed but jumped into his vehicle, made an illegal U-turn and sped off in the direction of the Maurice Bishop Highway. Sergeant Charles identified herself as a police officer and shouted after him to stop, but to no avail. She thought about shooting after the vehicle but she didn't want to endanger the civilians who were standing nearby. Besides, she didn't know why she was ordering him to stop. They could always catch him later. She looked down at her partner to seek answers.

Sergeant Jacob had reasonable cause to suspect that the young lady now sitting on the ground before him was carrying narcotics inside her shoes. He saw several white balls in the cavity of her platform heel. He now needed to secure the area. He called the uniformed officers to help secure a perimeter then summoned Corporal Sam on the radio who coincidentally had appeared through the automatic doors. Curious onlookers were gathering by now, forming a small crowd. Jacob ordered the woman to remove her shoes and he gave them to Sam. Her right ankle seemed swollen.

"Miss, you won't be travelling today," the sergeant assured the now distraught woman. "What's your name?"

The lady stared at Sergeant Jacob sullenly without responding. Sergeant Charles picked up the injured lady's handbag and retrieved her passport. It was British.

"Her passport say Bernadette Johnson-Penny," Charles said.

"Corporal, get some security officers and take this lady's luggage to the detention room," Sergeant Jacob ordered.

Sergeants Jacob and Charles and their detainee marched off to the detention room at the airport fire station to sort out the situation. This could be a long interview. A few minutes later, Corporal Sam and two security officers came in with three suitcases followed by Brian Griffith, the airport security manager.

"Mr. Griffith, make sure your people X-ray the shoes of every passenger that want to board that plane," Sergeant Charles instructed the security chief. "Check all platform shoes twice! They should be checked manually the second time."

Mr. Griffith thought about the delay the extra checks would cause and sighed. This could be another black mark on the efficiency of Grenada's airport security, he thought.

Half an hour later, a DS-1 pickup was speeding from the airport to the South St. George Police Station with the suspected drug trafficker. The agents needed to test and weigh the items found in her shoes, and question her further to build a strong case against her for drug trafficking. Johnson-Penny coming from Woburn, Sergeant Charles thought. Coincidence?

# CHAPTER 25

**Saturday October 26**
**5:30 a.m.**
**Woburn, St. George's**

The shrill tone of a cellphone alarm stabbed the stillness of the spacious bedroom in the west wing of the Johnson residence, prompting a massive paw to emerge from below the cover-sheet of the king size bed and search for the source of the annoying sound. The fingers of the right hand soon found the Samsung on the bedside table and successfully killed the noise. Big Daddy Johnson stretched lazily, his six-foot-five-inch, two hundred and eighty-five pound body taking up almost the entire bed. The sixty-six year old man always woke up at the same time and spent about fifteen minutes thinking about the state of his empire.

Aurelius Benedictus Johnson was actually born in Trinidad but was sent to Grenada by his mother in 1958 after he had used a stone to bash in the head of a schoolmate who had teased him about his name. Why had his mother cursed him with those strange Roman names? He had spent his teen years living in St. David's with his father. Soon after arriving in Grenada, everyone knew to avoid calling him by his given names. He was always big for his age, and would tower above his peers. It wasn't long before teenage girls in the neighbourhood were calling him "Big Daddy". Today, only his lawyer, his accountant and his bankers knew his official name. To everyone else, he was "Mr. Johnson". His twenty-four children from five different women all called him "Big Daddy". Seventeen of the children lived on the Woburn compound with him. He also allowed three of those women to stay on the compound. The youngest of the women, twenty-six, had his last child, aged four. He loved that boy to death. A smile crossed his face as he thought about his precious Bongani. Then he thought about Antonio, his oldest son living on the compound, and a frown replaced his smile.

Big Daddy sighed as he thought about the drive-by shooting that Antonio had pulled off at Progress Park. The boy had thought he had avenged his humiliation at the hands of the Alexander fellas, but all he had done was bring unnecessary attention to his family and their operations. He hoped that the vehicle they had used was burnt beyond recognition as Antonio had reported. Big Daddy stretched as he sat up in his bed, thinking about how he was forced to give his eldest son a "box" across his face for his stupidity. Had Antonio not been flesh and blood, he would've had him taken out to sea and left him to the sharks. His actions were definitely a setback to their operations.

Big Daddy thought about other setbacks they had recently experienced. These setbacks were costing him lots of money. The load he had sent off to Miami months ago was never collected and was eventually intercepted at MIA. His nephew who worked at the MBIA was investigated by the DIA for drug trafficking. The highly respected security officer finally decided to resign after having worked there for about twenty years. A few weeks ago, one of his daughters was caught at the airport with drugs in her shoes. He had come up with a fool-proof plan to pack platform shoe-bottoms with balls of cocaine to get the merchandise to England on trans-Atlantic flights. The inside of the platform bottoms was lined with material that hid the contents from X-ray machines. Now a few hundred thousand British pounds just went out the window! His lawyers would work out a deal to get his daughter a light sentence. She knew the risks.

The Johnson empire was collecting a tidy sum for the drugs they transported to North America and Europe. He needed to find ways to invest, use or hide all this money. So far, he was staying ahead of the "fast" FIU officers who were always snooping into his finances. His five-and-a-half-acre coastal compound had two mansions, a double-storey apartment building and some equipment sheds. His clan owned over twenty vehicles. Even his children's mothers each owned a car. The family also had four speedboats and two catamarans. Big Daddy laughed quietly as he thought about his investment in one of Grenada's biggest car dealerships. It was in the name of his half-brother, the independent member of parliament for St. David's, although the MP had only a 25% stake in the company. A closer look at the books of the car company would show that for a few years they had been depositing more money in banks than the dealership was actually making from selling cars. His brother didn't have a Master's degree in Accounting and Business Management for nothing. Hell, Big Daddy had even used some of the "dirty" money to make hefty contributions to the campaign of the member of parliament for the constituency in which he himself resided.

Johnson listened to dogs barking and nodded inwardly as he knew the fishermen were preparing to go raise their fish-pots offshore. He salivated as he imagined a steaming pot of fish broth for lunch. He made a mental note to have the boys go out and get some snapper for the ladies to cook. The animals in the village began stirring as birds chirped and sang excitedly, cocks crowed, sheep and goats bleated, and hens stretched their wings in flutters. As he thought about how his day would turn out, Big Daddy picked up an unfamiliar rumble from the bay outside his south window. He walked to the glass window and almost fainted when he pulled back the curtains. The grey steel hull of the Grenada Coast Guard Cutter *Victoria* loomed menacingly in the calm waters less than a kilometre offshore. Big Daddy's blurry vision also picked out three smaller grey boats, and hundreds of men clad in black scurrying along the jetty and shoreline looking like cockroaches under fluorescent light.

He ran to get his glasses and returned to the window to get a clearer view. He was only a bit relieved to see that what he thought were hundreds of men turned out to be about two or three dozen personnel. He knew his people could take care of them. He laughed scornfully and activated an alert from his cellphone.

# CHAPTER 26

At exactly 5:47 a.m., Assistant Commissioner of Police in charge of Operations, Jonathan Matthews, gave the order to commence Operation Fish Pot. He and Heads of the Special Services Unit, the Rapid Response Unit, the Drug Interdiction Agency and the Criminal Investigations Department had come up with a plan to execute warrants for the arrest of the suspects responsible for the drive-by shooting at Progress Park, and to search the premises for weapons and illegal drugs. It would be just like emptying a fish pot. The DIA, specifically DS-1, had made a series of breakthroughs in the war against White Spice in the past weeks, and investigations were pointing mainly to the Johnson family here in Woburn. The lawmen didn't expect this to be a piece of cake so they were pulling out all the stops to ensure the success of the mission.

Matthews sat in a green camouflaged Humvee Command and Communications vehicle a half-mile up the road from the main gate of the compound studying the layout of the five-and-a-half-acre property displayed on a Dell laptop. *Thank God for Google Earth*, he thought. He prayed that the men commanding each of the units involved in the operation would lead their respective teams well, and that casualties would be minimal if any. One hundred and sixty personnel were involved in the op – seventy-five SSU personnel, forty-five RRU commandos, and forty DIA agents. CID and FIU officers waited outside the compound until the place was secured.

The location of the compound on Grenada's southeast coast also warranted the participation of the Coast Guard. The Commissioner had authorised the use of four boats, including *Victoria*, as part of the operation.

Woburn Bay was a deep gash that was just one of several that scarred Grenada's southeastern Atlantic coastline. The entrance to the bay was guarded by Calivigny Resort Island to the north and Hog Island to the south. The Johnson compound occupied almost the entire length of the north shore of the bay. Pleasure yachts were berthed at Calivigny Resort Island while a few sailboats were anchored just offshore. Sailboats were also anchored around Hog Island. A few of the Johnson's boats were tied up at a jetty at the western-most end of the compound, in the inner bay.

From his vantage point on the road above the compound, Matthews thought that the place looked like a neat little college campus. Superintendent Grant of the SSU was sitting next to him and voiced that exact observation much to Matthews' surprise. Superintendent Duncan was also in the command vehicle and grunted in agreement. All three high-ranking officers were dressed in full combat gear including body armour. Duncan was dressed in black like his RRU personnel while the other two men wore green camouflage BDU's. The already muscular men now looked like professional bodybuilders. They scanned the three-D map of the compound on a monitor while discussing the best plan of attack. Someone had planned the layout of the property well. They admired the well-manicured lawns surrounding the buildings they could see. There were even parking lots with mostly SUV's occupying the spaces. The main road that snaked through the property was marked with a yellow line to make two lanes. They even saw a stop sign at an intersection. Matthews pressed a pair of binoculars to his eyes and whistled as he noted the expensive brands of the vehicles. There was a shiny black Hummer parked outside the grey mansion. No other vehicle was parked close to it. That was Big Daddy's ride.

The mansion itself looked like the letter B with the straight side of the building on the land side of the compound running almost parallel to the road on which they were parked, while the curved parts faced the waters of the bay. There was a courtyard where the curves of the B met in the middle. Staircases led from the courtyard to the first and second floors. Matthews knew that the ground floor contained storerooms and offices. His people would be thoroughly searching the entire building after they capture it. The assistant commissioner panned his glasses further east to observe an apartment building half-hidden by trees. All seemed to be quiet. Swinging west to where the bay ended and curved around to the south shore, he noted with satisfaction lawmen storming stealthily ashore. Two Defender-33 Coast Guard boats were ferrying personnel from the cutter *Victoria*, to the jetty.

The DIA agents in their dark blue combat fatigues, black helmets, black balaclava masks and protective goggles were already entering the sheds close to the jetty at the west end of the compound. Most of the twenty-five agents who breached the compound by boat carried Colt M4 assault rifles. Inspector Andrews and six DS-1 men brandished HK UMP9 submachine guns. Andrews ejected and checked his curved magazine for a third time before heading cautiously towards the grey mansion, their primary target. He looked up at the massive three-storey structure and thought how easy it would be for the Johnsons to ambush them. Each floor had a veranda along the entire south side, facing the Woburn Bay. The windows were far back from the edge of the veranda. All of them seemed to be tinted. He was glad that the men were all wearing dark goggles because the rising sun was reflecting off the mirrored glass windows and almost blinding anyone looking at the building from the south and east. If someone shot at them with a machine gun from the top floors, it would be hard for the lawmen to escape harm. He and his men were practically sitting ducks as they inched closer to the ground floor of the suspected drug don's lair. The inspector took solace in knowing that he had a sniper team on Hog Island, just over a kilometre offshore. He had confidence that Sergeant Jacob could take out any threat before that threat took them out as they crouched on the shores of Woburn Bay. Or he could have *Victoria* shoot up the house with its big guns.

Commandos of the RRU, wearing balaclava masks and armed with Colt M4 assault rifles were kicking in doors and identifying themselves even as Big Daddy was trying to raise the alarm that his kingdom was under attack. The green mansion about five hundred metres north of his house was captured without a shot being fired by anyone. The occupants were taken totally by surprise. On the ground floor, a half-naked young woman had made a dash for a gun hidden behind a toilet but a well-placed boot to her ankles had sent her screaming to the floor in agony before she even made it to the bathroom door. The occupants upstairs the main section of that building had groggily come out of their rooms to investigate the commotion only to be greeted by the business end of automatic rifles held by masked men dressed in black. The twelve commandos who stormed the building rounded up its eighteen occupants, including seven children, and herded them into one of the verandas on the northern side of the building. Each adult was handcuffed with plastic ties. Among them were four Hispanics – three males and a female. Sergeant George, the leader of the squad, radioed the police command vehicle to report that his building was secure.

On the easternmost edge of the compound, two squads of twelve RRU personnel each were breaching a green two-storey apartment building. The group had spent the night in the bushes outside the northeastern corner of the compound waiting for the hour to scale the ten-foot wall. Four-man teams each took one of the three flats on both floors, entering through main doors on the northern side. As one team kicked in the door to an upstairs apartment, a tall dread-locked man dove headfirst out of an open south window and heaved himself over the veranda. Corporal

Wendy James headed to the window, her rifle leading the way. She grunted indifferently as she saw the rastaman lying motionless in a pool of blood on the concrete pavement about twenty feet below. She noticed several SSU personnel covering that side of the building against any escape attempt by its occupants, gave a curt nod, and headed back indoors. The other commandos cleared and secured the apartment, ushering four screaming children and two women to a ground floor veranda. The other RRU teams were also bringing their detainees to the pre-planned holding area and cuffed each adult with plastic ties. One teenage boy suddenly rushed a couple of the steely-eyed officers, spitting out a string of expletives. A strong backhand hurled the boy back against his bound family members, his lips swelling rapidly. He spat out blood and a couple of teeth. He was promptly handcuffed.

"All-you better behave all-you self!" an officer warned the detainees gruffly. "Doh make me shoot all-you!"

The children became silent immediately. Some started shivering. Two officers went into the adjoining apartment to search for blankets and returned to hand them to the huddled children.

Automatic gunfire suddenly smashed the morning stillness, re-igniting a chorus of screams from the children. The women joined in the cacophony, much to the chagrin of the officers guarding them. None of the commandos moved a muscle as they exchanged glances. They knew that the firefight was taking place to the southwest of them, on the sea side of the compound. They were all safely on the land side. They were confident that their colleagues would deal with whatever threat existed over there.

In his command vehicle, ACP Matthews was moving his head back and forth with the binoculars, taking in the situation unfolding below his position. The squad of twelve SSU personnel that protected his Humvee fanned out, some looking down at the compound also while others faced the houses behind and above their position. Matthews noted that the fight seemed to be on the sea side of Big Daddy's mansion. He raised his gaze to check out

Calivigny Island just less than two kilometres to their north-east and hoped that the tourists at the luxury resort weren't filming the action on the mainland. Inspector Andrews and his men were taking heavy fire.

A total of ten men, armed with Uzi submachine guns, M-16's and an AK-47, were on the first and second floor verandas of the west wing of Big Daddy's house spraying the approaching lawmen with bullets. Two officers went down immediately, having caught rounds in their Kevlar protective vests. A couple of their comrades dragged them to safety, but one of the would-be rescuers was hit in the left arm as he moved backwards while dragging his comrade. A medic crawled to where they sought protection behind a Chevy pickup to patch them up. Inspector Andrews risked a peek around the back of the car that provided him with some cover and realised that the attackers were lying on the ground in the veranda shooting from between the concrete balusters. It would be hard for his men to eliminate them from this position. He lifted his weapon over car's trunk and blindly fired a burst at a spot where he estimated the enemy to be.

"We ha' to move!" he shouted above the incessant gunfire.

"You crazy?" screamed a wild-eyed DIA agent. "Dem men shooting back!"

Andrews looked at the scared man. None of the agents had ever been in a firefight before. They were used to everyone complying with their commands. Nobody usually resisted the personnel of the SSU, RRU or DIA. This situation was totally new to them. He observed other men, including some DS-1 agents, cowering behind the wheels of vehicles. He couldn't blame them. But this was not the time to be cowards. They had all signed up to defend the country.

"Fellas," he called out. "Ah calling for cover fire from the boats. When you hear they open up with the machine guns, we heading for the west corner of the house."

Heads nodded in acknowledgement. Andrews spoke briefly into

his radio with ACP Matthews. A minute later, the heavy thumping of M60 machine guns reached the pinned lawmen as both Defender-33 boats in the bay opened up mercilessly on the ambushers in the mansion. Concrete disintegrated as 7.62 mm NATO rounds ripped up the balusters, sending splinters into the faces and eyes of the men lying prone on the floor. The ten attackers retreated into the house. One man on the second floor carelessly stood up to run inside and was decapitated immediately, his lifeless body taking a half-step before collapsing to the tiled floor.

Keeping low, Andrews and his men ran full speed towards the building. A few of them fired up at the first floor while on the run. A couple of agents completed the dash by executing a dive and shoulder roll over the final four metres. They pressed themselves against the west wall, away from the line of fire from the verandas. As the inspector leaned against the wall to catch his breath, a message came through his earpiece saying that the east wing of the mansion was secured. *Now comes the fun part*, Andrews thought, as he formulated a plan to infiltrate the west wing to capture Big Daddy and his boys.

# CHAPTER 27

The village of Woburn awoke to the sounds of automatic rifles and heavy machine guns, and some of its inhabitants immediately started calling 911. Some villagers older than forty years had flashbacks of the American-led invasion in 1983 and cowered below beds and inside closets and cupboards. Teenagers headed to high ground above the action to take pictures and shoot videos with their smartphones and digital cameras. Everyone was surprised to see police vehicles everywhere. The entire village was cordoned off from the outside world. Less than twenty minutes after the gunfight began, footage began to flow into Facebook, Twitter and YouTube.

ACP Matthews now had to contend with civilians potentially getting into harm's way in addition to overseeing the operation. He hadn't expected the Johnsons to resist to this extent. He smiled inwardly as he thought how wise it was for them to have the Coast Guard provide support from offshore. *Victoria* could use its M242 chain gun, if needed, to pound those slackers into submission. The police would pick up the pieces later. He had noted with satisfaction how effectively the Defender boats were providing cover fire with their machine guns for the DIA agents as the latter tried to get to Big Daddy's house. He knew that there were no children in that building; Big Daddy only allowed his sons and some of his nephews to live there. According to the intelligence gathered, up to twelve males lived in the mansion. Some of them probably had their women with them. The don himself occupied the entire second floor of the west wing of the B-shaped mansion. Matthews ordered Superintendent Grant to dispatch some SSU personnel to get the inquisitive teenagers on the hill to safety.

Fresh gunfire erupted, this time from the northeastern end of the compound. Matthews knew that his people didn't carry the weapons he was hearing.

"Where that coming from?" the ACP asked his young communications officer.

The corporal circled an area of the map on the computer monitor somewhere between Big Daddy's house and the apartment building. That area seemed to be a wooded section of the property.

"It look like people coming from around there," she said.

"Dammit!" Matthews swore. "This map is outdated."

He picked up a briefcase.

"Time to break out the Hornet," he grinned at Corporal LaTouche.

The PD-100 is an unmanned air vehicle ten centimetres long that weighs sixteen grams, even with its three surveillance cameras. In April of this year, the British government had donated the system to the RGPF to help in the war against White Spice. The police hierarchy was elated to have this gift as it gave the DIA an added advantage in surveillance and intelligence gathering. The tiny drone could send back live video images to its operator. Corporal LaTouche looked at the toy in Matthews' hand. She had never seen it before.

"Sir, what you going to do with that?"

"We need eyes on the battlefield," he replied. "We have to see what's between those trees and direct our men there."

He could hear M4 rifles returning fire.

"SIR, CONTACT WITH SOME SPANISH MEN! TAKING HEAVY FIRE!"

Matthews recognised Sergeant George's voice bellowing in his headset, gunfire in the background. The ACP could only surmise that "Spanish men" meant South Americans, most likely Venezuelans or Colombians.

"We sending backup now!" Matthews yelled into his comm set.

Superintendent Grant ordered fifteen SSU personnel to join the fight in the woods of the compound. Matthews then deployed the UAV to give them an eye in the sky. He spoke to Sergeant George.

"Sarge, how many bad guys?"

Sergeant George answered haltingly, his heavy breathing giving Matthews an idea of the intensity of the battle he was engaged in. "Ah not sure. Maybe ten."

Matthews sped the drone to the latest battlefield. The colour monitor of the UAV system showed some brown-skinned and Caucasian individuals dressed in jeans and t-shirts shooting at several RRU personnel. His men were pinned down in the veranda of the green mansion. He wondered why foreigners would attack that building when it was controlled by the police. Maybe they have a stash of money there. He consulted briefly with Superintendent Duncan. Duncan keyed his radio to speak to Bravo Squad leader at the apartment building further east.

"Sergeant Thomas, move your men to take up a position behind those bandits and engage."

Thomas acknowledged the order and led his men stealthily through the brush and woods to take on the South Americans. He would prefer to take them alive but he didn't think it was necessary.

"Fellas, we wiping out dem men," he said grimly as they crouched low to discuss how they would engage the foreigners. He ordered one man to climb a huge cedar tree to provide cover fire for the men on the ground. The tree gave the man a direct line of fire to most of the bandits who had their backs turned to them less than one hundred metres away. Keeping low, five commandos moved towards the seaside so as to stay out of the line of fire from their colleagues firing from the veranda of the green mansion. Thomas and the remaining men headed to the north wall. The bandits were now surrounded.

“Drop your weapons and put your hands up!” Sergeant Thomas commanded loudly.

Two of the Hispanic men whirled around, raising HK 416 automatics. They held the triggers down as they fired in the direction of Sergeant Thomas’ voice. The Grenadian officer and two other commandos beside him hugged the ground, rolling away from the incoming lethal projectiles. The lawmen could hear the 5.56 mm NATO rounds cut through the brush above them like a scythe. Short bursts from an M4 silenced the HK sub-machine guns and the commandos heard a couple of thuds. They hoped the bad guys were dead. There was another short burst from the M4 in the tree followed by loud screaming and cursing in Spanish. Thomas could hear Grenadian accents shouting amid the intermittent gunfire in the woods. The SSU personnel had arrived to provide support. He called out to them, identifying himself and his men. He looked at the wounded Hispanic.

“Medic!” he called out.

Soon the foreigner’s wounded leg was being patched up. The lawmen were glad to get at least one prisoner.

“Where the other Spanish men?” Sergeant George asked, panting heavily. He had just run up from his veranda of refuge.

“Man, you really outta shape,” Sergeant Thomas snorted scornfully at his colleague.

George steupsed loudly, glaring at Thomas.

They heard shouting and the reports of pistols and rifle fire followed by more yells and howls. The other South Americans were trying to escape but were captured by the rest of Sergeant Thomas’ squad. The sound of boots approached from the direction of the sea and voices called out so that Thomas and the other RRU and SSU personnel wouldn’t fire on their comrades. Six sullen Hispanic men emerged through the brush, some of them sporting swollen and bloodied faces. Thomas and George exchanged knowing glances but said nothing. They needed to get these foreigners off the compound right now. They apprised ACP Matthews of the situation. Superintendent Grant ordered some of the SSU personnel to escort the seven prisoners to the staging area outside the compound. Duncan commanded Sergeant Thomas to take his team to the southwestern side of the grey mansion to help Inspector Andrews and his agents capture Big Daddy and his boys. The ACP had no time for a long siege. He needed to secure that mansion and the entire compound as soon as possible.

# CHAPTER 28

Big Daddy sat on the floor of the living room in his second floor lair holding an unfired M16 rifle and panting heavily. He looked like he had just run a mile in dead sand. Two of his sons and three nephews were sitting with him. They all had their backs against the thick south wall, the shot-out veranda windows above their heads. Big Daddy realised he was losing his empire quickly. He hadn't expected the police to capture most of his compound so quickly. The RRU, SSU and DIA personnel had moved decisively to capture most of the buildings on the property. Only his personal mansion was still not totally under the control of the lawmen. He wondered what had happened to the Venezuelans who had been staying here for the last few days. They were supposed to be highly trained ex-soldiers. He had listened to the intense firefight coming from the woods between his house and the apartment complex a few minutes ago. But now there was silence, punctuated now and then by men screaming in pain, and curses in Spanish. The Woburn don sighed quietly as he concluded that the Venezuelans had been neutralised. He assessed his own situation.

Antonio and his brother, Joe, were trembling, their faces and shoulders bloodied by shards of concrete after the encounter with the machine guns of the Coast Guard boats. The body of their other brother, Kendall, was lying in the veranda, half of his head gone. Three of their cousins were also wounded including Damion who had caught a bullet to his hip and was whimpering as he sat in a pool of blood in a corner. Big Daddy crawled over to him to check the wound. It looked bad. Four of his nephews who were firing on the invading lawmen from the first floor had come up to the second floor via an internal staircase. Their breathing was pregnant with anxiety and fear. They could not escape via the fire escape on the north side of the building. SSU personnel covered every possible exit.

"All-you, doh worry," the don reassured the young men. "For dem men to come up here they have to climb the steps. We have higher ground. They kyant reach us without losing a lotta men."

"Big Daddy, you forget dem boats out there with their machine guns?" Antonio said. "They win already."

Big Daddy looked at his son, half in anger and half in sadness. All of this was his fault. But he would protect his son with his own life. He had no doubt that the police were here for Antonio. He couldn't understand why the DIA fellas were here, however. He had been very careful with his drug trafficking business. Then he remembered the capture of his son during a drug buy on the seas, and the arrest of his daughter at MBIA with stuff in her shoes. He groaned.

"Listen!" Joe whispered loudly.

"… OF THE RGPF. CEASE FIRE AND COME OUT WITH YOUR HANDS UP. YOU ARE SURROUNDED. WE HAVE A WARRANT TO SEARCH THE PREMISES AND FOR THE ARREST OF ANTONIO JOHNSON."

It was the voice of ACP Matthews from the road overlooking the compound.

Five pair of eyes looked intently at Big Daddy for directions. The young men wanted to surrender. They would take their chances in prison. But they doubted that Big Daddy would even consider giving up.

"Ah hope all-you know we not giving up," Big Daddy confirmed their suspicions. "We fighting to the last man."

The east wing of his mansion was already in the hands of the lawmen, but the police seemed to be stumped about how to reach the last holdout here in the west wing. Big Daddy had a plan. He crawled across to his bedroom and returned a couple minutes later dragging a cylindrical object. It was a rocket launcher.

"We ha' to take out dem boats," he announced. "Somebody will go out and fire two rockets and blow up dem Coast Guard speed boat. Then we go rush outside and kill the rest ah dem police."

The fellas realised that the person who fires the rockets would most likely be killed. They didn't dare ask who would get that task. Silence permeated the room.

"YOU HAVE ONE MINUTE!" came the voice over the bullhorn again.

"Gimme the damn weapon!" hissed Damion. "Ah dead already anyway!"

Big Daddy didn't even pretend to wait to be persuaded. He wasn't going to choose one of his sons for that job. But he couldn't decide which of his nephews to order to go out on the veranda to fire on the boats. He was relieved that the wounded Damion had volunteered. He made a show of thanking his nephew profusely for his sacrifice as he showed him how to use the weapon. The other guys were weeping as they realised that this was a suicide mission. Damion crawled to the door with the rocket launcher and two rockets.

**6:40 a.m.**
**Sauteurs, St. Patrick's**

Kellon Alexander sat at the dining table, sipping a cup of hot coffee, a plate with coconut bakes and saltfish in front of him. He was thumbing through his Samsung phone, looking at the latest feeds on his Facebook page. He looked at a very recent picture of some men in black combat fatigues engaged in a firefight. More violence in Trinidad, he thought. He continued scrolling and paid closer attention to similar pictures. What the hell!

"Junior!" he called out to his cousin.

Junior ran downstairs just as Kellon was heading to the Dell desktop in the living room.

"What happen?" Junior enquired.

"You would never believe wha' dey on Facebook."

Kellon turned on the computer and loaded his page. They were greeted with even more recent pictures of current military action somewhere in the Caribbean, and a short video.

"Where dat is?" Junior asked. "Jamaica?

"Boy that is right here in Grenada," Kellon replied. "Da is in Woburn!"

They looked at the video which was shot from above. Someone had captured the action from a drone. They watched the recording of two Defender-33 boats firing non-stop on a big grey house in Woburn Bay.

"Da is not dem Johnson place?" Kellon wondered aloud.

"Yep," Junior answered matter-of-factly.

They played the video three times. They recognised the uniforms of the RRU, SSU and DIA as men were sprinting from cover to cover, firing towards the grey house. The op seemed to be very well planned. It was just like a movie.

The cousins looked at each other in horror, both men thinking the same thing. They needed to get out of the drug business for good. They had a stash of merchandise in Frequente that they needed to move fast. But they knew that this wasn't the time. They were sure that they were being watched closely. They started discussing a timetable for getting rid of all the White Spice in their possession once and for all.

## Hog Island

Sergeant Jacob stretched out on his stomach on the ground of the small hill on Hog Island directly across from the Johnson compound in Woburn Bay. He had spent the night with his team on this offshore island so that they wouldn't be seen crossing the bridge at the break of dawn this morning to take up a position to cover the operation taking place right now. His mission was to provide cover fire from afar. His spotter, Sergeant Micky Davis, was lying next to him watching the compound to their north through powerful glasses. Six other heavily armed SSU personnel were fanned out to protect them from any threat from the west, south and east.

Jacob had chosen the McMillan TAC-50 sniper rifle for the operation. With its five-round detachable box magazine, the manually-operated bolt-action rifle had a range of about two kilometres. This weapon was originally intended to engage and disable light armoured vehicles but the ace sniper needed it today to cover the distance from Hog Island to the compound along the coastline across the bay. The sergeant sincerely hoped that he wouldn't have to engage a human target with this weapon because it would totally tear up a body.

"Target!" Sergeant Davis called out dryly.

Jacob always wondered how Davis could appear to be so calm whenever there was a possible human target in a mission like this one. They had done several ops together in training missions in South America. He aimed his scope at the area where the spotter indicated and almost stopped breathing. A wounded man in the grey mansion had a rocket launcher on his shoulder and was aiming it at the Interceptor boats in the bay. Jacob knew men on those boats. His scope was powerful enough for him to recognise the M72 LAW rocket launcher. Where were these people getting such weapons? The Force didn't even have rocket launchers. The man had trouble standing steady but he had propped himself against one of the cylindrical uprights in the veranda. Davis called out data so that the sniper could make adjustments for wind, spin drift and bullet drop as the projectile would streak across the bay towards its target. Jacob noticed that the wounded man had his entire body facing him. The bare-back man was just over a kilometre away from Hog Island. *Good boy*, he thought, as he aimed for centre mass. He knew he had little time to spare. He attempted to lower his heart rate by engaging in tactical breathing. Then he squeezed the trigger between heartbeats.

Travelling at a velocity of eight hundred and twenty-three metres per second, the .50 BMG cartridge flew across the bay tearing into Damion Johnson's upper chest 1.3 seconds after it left Hog Island. The impact slammed his body into the back wall of the veranda as a massive hole appeared in his left peck. The doomed young man had managed to fire the rocket just as the bullet tore open his chest, causing the boats in the bay to frantically take evasive action as they tried to create more space between them and the approaching missile. The pilot of the closer boat tried to move deeper into the bay and slammed the throttle forward to pick up speed, while turning sharply to port. The machine gunner was caught off-guard and was thrown overboard. The rocket slammed into the cabin of the other Defender boat, exploding on impact. The pilot and a sailor inside the cabin were killed instantly, but the machine gunner had seen the streaking rocket and had thrown himself overboard a second before impact. The concussion from the explosion had rendered him unconscious before he hit the water. Another sailor was seriously wounded from the blast, his bloodied frame floating on the surface of the now oily water. The undamaged boat pulled around to pick up its gunner and assist the wounded men from the crippled Defender. Within a minute, *Victoria* had dispatched its RIB with a rescue team to the scene.

Matthews and his officers watched in horror from their vantage point on the hill as one of the Defender boats was all but destroyed. Even from that distance they could hear screams of pain floating across the bay as the wounded sailor bawled for his mother. About eight hundred metres offshore, the .50 calibre machine gun on *Victoria* opened up as Captain Aberdeen gave the order to pepper the top floor of Big Daddy's house with lead. The concrete walls of the house provided little resistance against the projectiles from the heavy machine gun. Obviously Aberdeen had revenge on his mind and didn't intend to let anyone leave that house alive. But the commissioner had ordered that they try hard to capture Antonio and Big Daddy alive. Matthews radioed the captain of *Victoria* to cease fire.

Inspector Andrews and Sergeant Thomas took advantage of the sudden lull in fire from *Victoria* to race up the steps with their men to get to the Johnsons holed up on the second floor. While Thomas' squad checked the first floor, Andrews led a dozen personnel to the top floor. They were shocked at the carnage that greeted them on the veranda. Two commandos crawled over the headless body of Damion Johnson to the shot-out windows of the living-room. Each tossed a concussion grenade in different directions into the massive room. They laid flat on the ground and covered their ears as the grenades exploded. Howls and screams erupted as the "flash-bangs" disoriented the men inside. Thirteen lawmen rushed into the room shouting at nine individuals who were writhing on the floor, clawing blindly at the air, blood oozing from their ears. Some of the commandos moved to check the other rooms for more occupants and returned to report that the place was clear. Inspector Andrews radioed ACP Matthews that they had captured Antonio Johnson and his father and brother, among others. Five minutes later, Matthews himself appeared to officially arrest the Johnsons. Ambulances sped them off to the hospital under escort by a heavily armed security detail.

Within ten minutes, detectives from CID and investigators of the

FIU were swarming the compound gathering evidence for their respective investigations. ACP Matthews could hardly believe the amount of cocaine and cash they found on the compound. He decided to load the drugs onto *Victoria* to take back to the Coast Guard base in True Blue. He and Inspector Andrews estimated that they had captured about two tonnes of cocaine and over twelve million American dollars in cash. This was a huge victory for the police in the war on White Spice. The lawmen also found several caches of weapons, including sophisticated arms that not even the RGPF had in its arsenal. Matthews shook hands with the heads of the SSU and RRU as they considered the success of the operation.

"If the commissioner run for election right now, she winning in a landslide," Superintendent Duncan joked.

The officers laughed heartily.

# CHAPTER 29

**Saturday December 21**
**9:40 p.m.**
**Frequente, St. George's**

Kellon loaded the last of the eleven boxes into the back of the van and shut the door. He softly dusted his palms against each other and looked around to see if they were being observed. He and Junior had decided to move the stash of cocaine from its temporary storage in one of their apartment buildings in Frequente, to a building they owned in Victoria, St. Mark's. They had been shaken by the decisive action taken by the Drug Interdiction Agency and paramilitary units of the RGPF a couple months ago against the Johnson clan in Woburn. The raid on the sprawling compound, and the subsequent firefight had left four of Johnson's people dead, along with two law enforcement personnel. It was the worse gun battle in Grenada's history since October 1983. The raid had netted millions of American dollars in cash, dozens of high powered weapons, and tonnes of cocaine, according to police reports. The commissioner was not joking when she spoke about killing drug trafficking in the country. That breakthrough had prompted the Alexander cousins to take the decision to move their merchandise to new storage facilities every couple weeks until they got rid of it once and for all.

"Man, you sure it won't have much police on the road?" Junior asked anxiously.

December was always a busy time of the year and there was sure to be a lot of traffic on the road on this Saturday night.

"Trust me," Kellon reassured his cousin. "Dem police busy tonight."

"I really hope so. We carrying a lot of stuff. If we get caught, we not seeing outside Richmond Hill prison again."

Kellon laughed.

"Dem men maybe drunk all now," he replied, slapping his cousin on the back.

He climbed into the driver's seat of their white 1990's Chevrolet G-series van while Junior jumped into the front passenger seat. He hated operating left-hand drive vehicles on Grenada's roads. He could never see around stopped vehicles in his lane in order to pass them. He often wondered why the government didn't ban the importation of left-hand drive vehicles. They had imported this van in 2007 after buying it very cheaply in Florida. The registration had expired about two years ago, and they hadn't insured it since that time. Only the driver had a seat belt, and the right headlamp wasn't working. Using their new Hummer for tonight's mission was out of the question. Junior had suggested using one of the company trucks to transport the contraband, but he didn't want to risk tarnishing the company's name if they got caught. He chuckled as he thought about the myriad of charges they would have to face if they were ever caught tonight.

"So where we passing to reach Victoria?" Junior asked as they pulled onto the Maurice Bishop highway to head north.

"We'll go through Grand Anse then hit the Western Main Road."

"You crazy?" Junior was alarmed. "You plan to pass in the middle of town?"

"Nah man," Kellon replied calmly. "Cool down, we not going through the city."

Junior heaved a sigh of relief.

"Relax, Cuz. Everything under control." Kellon grinned at his cousin, glancing at him for a second and reaching over to slap him on the shoulder.

"Look out!" Junior yelled.

Kellon's attention snapped back to the road to see a Grand Anse bus suddenly stop in front of him. He blew his horn angrily and swerved right to avoid running into the back of the white Toyota Hiace. He swore in Spanish, thanking his lucky stars that there were two north-bound lanes on this part of the highway, and the fast lane was open.

"These busmen really putting people life in danger!" Kellon exclaimed. His palms were wet and he was sweating after that close call.

"Drive carefully," Junior pleaded. "We can't afford to get stop for a traffic violation tonight."

"Man, cool it, nuh!" Kellon snapped, still shaken. "I tell you dem police not studying people tonight."

He pulled into a gas station to put $40 worth of gas into the vehicle. The extra two and a half gallons should get them to Sauteurs after the Victoria stop. Ten minutes later, they were driving through Grand Anse on their way to the Western Main Road.

Inspector Andrews drove the black Isuzu D-Max pickup southward along the Grand Anse main road, muttering to himself about the heavy traffic at this time of night. The heavily tinted windows were up, and the a/c was running at almost maximum. He looked at the clock on the dashboard for the hundredth time, wondering if they would make it in time to get some food. Tonight was the annual SSU Christmas party at Camp Salines. It was expected to be blessed with foods and drinks of all kinds. He was particularly interested in the lambie waters, as were most of the men in the Force. He could care less for the baked chicken, macaroni pie, rice and peas, stewed pork and fried jacks. The wide variety of food as well as the abundance of alcohol attracted the men and women of the Force from all over the country. Even those who were on duty found some time to pass by for a bite.

"Man, I just hope it still have *manicou*," a female voice rang out from the seat behind the inspector. Corporal Peters would never pass up a good portion of stewed opossum.

"How all-you could really eat that?" Sergeant Jacob asked rhetorically. He was sitting beside Andrews, glaring at the car in front of them.

"Inspeck, why you don't put on the siren?" Jacob finally suggested. "We could pass all these cars and reach in time to get more than just left overs."

"True," Andrews agreed. "But since when rushing for food is a legit emergency?"

Peters sighed in frustration as they stopped for a red light at the Food Fair junction.

"Where all these people come from?" she wondered aloud, as dozens of pedestrians crossed the intersection.

The traffic light turned green and they continued in the long line of vehicles. Buses were whizzing by in the opposite direction at top speed, carrying passengers to St. George's. A convoy of four motorbikes roared past the line of south-bound vehicles, weaving between cars to avoid oncoming traffic.

"Dem fellas have a death wish?" Andrews growled. He secretly envied them at that very moment. That was what he needed in this traffic. But he preferred the protection that four-wheel vehicles provided drivers and passengers.

"I sure that is Fratty an' dem," Corporal Peters remarked confidently. "They better leave food for us."

"Is he self," Jacob grumbled. "Dem fellas could real eat."

Earlier that night, the three officers had been delayed in Gouyave as they dealt with a drug trafficking case involving a fishing boat from that west coast town. The captain of the boat was helping them with their investigation, but he was not cooperating fully. The police had found out that the owner of the boat was a well-known entertainer. But nobody owned up to the twenty kilogrammes of cocaine that was discovered in the trawler. The captain and his two crewmen could only be detained for forty-eight hours before they had to be released, unless evidence was found to connect them to the illegal drugs. Inspector Andrews and his team had tried their best to retrace the path of the boat over the past forty-eight hours. They gave up after two hours. Let the three men spend the night in the cell. They had a fete to get to all the way in the south of the island.

The pickup crested the slope at Excel Plaza and headed to the Republic House round-about.

"Rhatid!!"

The Jamaican expletive exploded from Sergeant Jacob's mouth as a white, old American-model van suddenly appeared from behind a stopped minibus, taking up their space in the south-bound lane. There was no room for Inspector Andrews to avoid a head-on collision.

"God!" Andrews shouted as he geared down from fourth to second while slamming on the brake. The wheels locked causing the tyres to screech loudly on the pavement. Momentum carried the unmarked police vehicle towards the approaching van. Corporal Peters screamed. There was no escape. The bull bar at the front of the D-Max slammed into the front of the Chevrolet in a sickening metallic crunch. The impact sent the van into the stationary bus, causing passengers to scream hysterically. The airbags in the police vehicle activated, saving the inspector and the sergeant from slamming their heads onto the steering wheel and dashboard. Peters wasn't wearing her seat belt and her body lurched forward violently, her head hitting the headrest of the driver's seat hard. She blacked out for a few seconds. Even with the windows turned up and his face buried in the airbag, Andrews heard the unmistakable crack of bone followed by howling as the right side of the police pickup – his side – slammed into the young bus-driver's arm that was dangling outside as the would-be Casanova was flirting with a female passenger twice his age.

"Everybody OK?" Andrews inquired of his team.

Sergeant Jacob freed himself from his airbag and looked behind the driver's seat to check on Corporal Peters. She groaned loudly and rubbed her neck. She was still groggy.

"I good," Jacob announced. "But Peters look like she need help.

"Peters, stay here while I go and check out things!" Andrews ordered. "Come with me, Sergeant."

The men put on their black DIA-inscribed caps to head outside. Andrews had to exit using the front passenger side. Both men gasped as they took in the scene.

# CHAPTER 30

Screaming, howling, flashing lights, and the incessant yapping of voices bombarded Kellon's senses as he regained consciousness. He was grateful for his seatbelt. He shook his head to clear the stars, but the flashing lights continued. Then he realised that the lights were from people's cellphone cameras as they captured the accident to upload to Facebook and Twitter. He had a throbbing headache. He had knocked his head hard against the steering wheel. His right arm was aching like nothing he had ever experienced before. He looked at it and realised that it was hanging limply. It was broken!

"Junior, you alive, boy?" he croaked weakly, looking to his right at his cousin.

Kellon almost passed out again as he saw the top half of Junior's body dangling through the shattered windshield. He bawled out and reached awkwardly to pull his cousin back in the vehicle with his left hand. A stabbing pain in his mid-section slammed him back into his seat and he screamed in agony. He glared at the wide-bodied white Toyota bus that took up the entire north-bound lane and wished he could shoot the driver. That fool just killed his cousin! What was he going to tell Jeffrey? A figure wearing a black cap was approaching his van. As the body drew closer, he realised that it was a police officer. And the cap had the DIA insignia in reflective white on it! He passed out again.

"All-you OK inside dey?" Inspector Andrews shouted towards

the van, concern in his voice. He could detect no movement coming from inside the large vehicle.

There was no reply. He ordered Sergeant Jacob to call for ambulances, Fire/Rescue and police units. He checked the bus. A few passengers had some minor scrapes but the driver had a broken arm. He was also trapped in the vehicle. The right front corner of the bus was wrapped around his feet and legs. It was likely that they were broken as well. The young man was bawling incessantly, asking the female passenger with whom he had been flirting if he would die. By now, all the other passengers were standing outside the bus, some shocked, some angry, some whimpering and some crying.

Jacob appeared with Corporal Peters by his side. She was carrying a first-aid kit.

"How are you, Corporal?" Inspector Andrews asked her, looking at her closely.

"I'll live."

Andrews nodded, acknowledging Peters' bravery.

"Check the people in that van," he said to her. "I find that passenger looking like he badly hurt."

After a few seconds, Peters reported that the passenger of the van was deceased. She checked the driver and swore under her breath.

"Inspector," she called out. "I think you want to see this."

Inspector Andrews raced to Peters and found her holding up the head of Kellon Alexander. His eyes bulged with surprise. He looked at the van, noting its dilapidated state and expired registration sticker, then looked at his watch, and whistled. A theory was forming in his mind.

"He alive?" he asked the junior officer.

"Yes, Sir."

Inspector Andrews thought about the scene before them then placed a call to base. He knew he would be interrupting the SSU Christmas party but this could be the big break they needed.

Ten minutes after the horrific collision, the accident scene was crawling with six other DS-1 agents, eight police officers from the Traffic Department, a Fire/Rescue unit, and several medical personnel in four ambulances. The Fire/Rescue unit had to use the jaws-of-life to extricate the driver of the bus. An undertaker also arrived to deal with Junior Alexander's body. Traffic officers redirected traffic to other routes to ease the congestion that had inevitably taken place. Inspector Andrews consulted with the lead officer.

"Inspector Gabriel, that van may contain illegal drugs," Andrews pointed towards the white Chevrolet. "We have to search it."

"Andrews, you just can't search the van so," Gabriel growled, shaking his head in disapproval.

Andrews pulled Gabriel aside to apprise him of who the occupants of the van were. Gabriel looked at his colleague long and hard then sighed, shaking his head like a defeated man.

"Well," he began. "The van is not licensed so it most likely not insured too. If we find this vehicle not insured, we have to take it in."

"These men are suspected drug dealers," Andrews pressed. "That should give us enough grounds to search the vehicle."

Inspector Gabriel smiled.

"Why drug dealers driving ah unlicense ol' van with one headlamp so late in the night, on a night when most police officers at the SSU Christmas fete?" the Traffic officer wondered, pulling his round chin.

"Exactly!" Inspector Andrews whispered, smiling.

"You better thank that busman for stopping off a bus stop," Gabriel remarked. "But we still go have to charge him."

Andrews signalled to one of his agents to search the van. At the same time he was alerted to a commotion at the old van. Kellon had regained consciousness and was becoming agitated as two DS-1 agents approached the back of the vehicle. He was struggling with Corporal Peters and a nurse as they attended to his wounds.

"What all-you doing?" Kellon rasped, fighting for breath. "You have no right! I will sue all-you for invasion of privacy. Get away!"

The two inspectors exchanged glances and moved toward the back of the van to peer inside the vehicle.

"Wait! Dah is dem Sauteurs drugmen," a bystander shouted.

"Ah sure is drugs dem have inside dey," a female voice opined confidently.

Blackberries, Samsungs, Nokias and other mobile devices flashed as people tried to record the possible capture of one of the country's biggest suspected drug dealers.

Andrews ordered the police officers to try to disperse the small crowd. Kellon made an attempt to run. He collapsed on his broken right ankle after half a step. He coughed a couple times, blood dribbling down his chin. Two officers lifted and half-carried him to the ambulance. They watched him closely as the nurse continued to tend to him. They were very surprised when he suddenly broke down and started to cry.

"Ah sorry, Jeffrey," he blubbered over and over again.

"Look at this," Agent Sam called out from the old Chevy. He was holding up a 9 mm pistol in his right hand by the butt with his thumb and forefinger. "I found it below the driver seat."

"Bag it," Andrews ordered. He recalled the 9 mm shell casings that were found on Levera Beach months ago. He called on Jacob to bring the mobile drug testing kit to the van.

All the agents were staring at the boxes stacked neatly inside the van. Even the jolt from the crash hadn't moved them much. The agents concluded that they contained stuff that weighed a lot. Sergeants Jacob and Charles donned gloves and started opening boxes. Each contained transparent plastic bags of a white powdery substance. Charles began to test a few samples from several boxes.

"Well we can safely say dem fellas not going and bake Christmas cake tonight," she joked. "This stuff is not flour; it's White Spice!"

Inspector Andrews heaved a sigh of relief as he felt vindicated for what most people thought was his team's harassment of the Alexander boys. He used his cell phone to shoot video of the open boxes then ordered that they be loaded onto a pickup to be taken to base for storage.

"I'm going to enjoy this," he said smugly to his team. He beckoned them to follow him to the lone ambulance left on the scene.

As Kellon laid in the back of the ambulance, he was shocked to see six DS-1 agents walking towards him, all of them packing side-arms. Inspector Andrews was even grinning broadly. The injured man began sweating nervously, and the nurse, Millette, thought that he was having a cardiac event. She turned around to see the police officers.

"All-you crazy," she shouted at the approaching anti-narcotics agents. "You want to raise the man pressure and kill him?"

Inspector Andrews ignored her and addressed Kellon.

"Mr. Alexander, you are under arrest for drug possession with intent to traffic."

He read Kellon his rights, smirking, as the once king of Sauteurs was now sobbing.

Two major drug busts within months! Not bad!

Inspector Andrews and his team sat on a low wall at the side of the road, thinking about their major achievements in the war against White Spice over the past year. He thought about the long meetings to come with the Superintendent Telesford, the commissioner, and the prime minister. He suddenly stood up, stretched, and walked towards one of the vehicles that came from Camp Salines.

"All-you not hungry or wha'?" he shouted to his people.

The agents forgot about the bust momentarily as they thought about the Christmas fete. They watched as a police tow-truck pulled the uninsured Chevy van back to the SSU camp. The tow-truck would return for Andrews' banged-up pickup. The inspector and five other DS-1 agents piled into the pickup with the seized cocaine and sped off to Camp Salines to hopefully get some leftovers from the Christmas fete.

# EPILOGUE

**New Year's Eve**
**1:50 p.m.**
**SSU Camp, Point Salines**

Inspector Ricky Andrews stormed into the DS-1 squad room holding a huge bowl of peas soup. Steam lifted from the enamel container as the top anti-narcotics agent hurriedly and carefully placed the hot bowl on a table. A couple of other agents checked out his food and noted the dumplings, salt-beef, sweet potatoes, pig tail, yam and green bananas that barely floated among the pigeon peas in the soup.

"She start yet?" Andrews asked anxiously.

The squad was assembled around the TV monitor to look at a live press conference given by Commissioner Coutain as she addressed and evaluated the war on White Spice for the past twelve months.

"She start five minutes ago," Sergeant Charles replied.

"But, Inspeck, you take all the food, man!" Sergeant Jacob needled his commanding officer. "What you expect the rest of us to get?"

"Go in the canteen and see if it still have in the pot," Andrews said. "But doh expect to get plenty dumpling."

Laughter erupted in the squad room. Everyone knew that Andrews had a weakness for dumplings in peas soup and oil-down.

"Everybody here?" the inspector inquired.

"Nah," Corporal Peters answered. "Sam and Smith on the airport now."

"We expecting a flight this afternoon?" Andrews asked in surprise.

"British Airways coming in soon," Peters responded.

Inspector Andrews grunted as he acknowledged the reply. They always had to be very vigilant with these British flights. About ninety percent of the suspected drug mules this year were associated with British flights. The DIA had decided to deploy a K-9 unit to the airport to help DS-1 sniff out the would-be traffickers.

"All-you, hush," someone called out. "She talking about us now."

Silence floated over the room as all eyes focused on the television. Commissioner Coutain was giving her press conference at the RGPF headquarters at Fort George in St. George's. She was dressed in her khaki uniform, sitting erect at the table. The Deputy Commissioner was at her left side, his expressionless eyes staring straight into the camera directly in front of them. Superintendent Telesford sat at her right, scrolling through a laptop as he was getting a slideshow ready to present to the media.

"Man, you could never read Mr. David eyes," Peters remarked.

Commissioner Coutain was at the moment reading statistics about the amount of cocaine confiscated in six operations during the year, including the major load captured in Woburn at the Johnson compound; and the contraband confiscated from the Alexanders as they transported it along the Grand Anse road on December 21. The DS-1 team was surprised to learn that the total amount of White Spice captured in 2013 had a value of just over three hundred and fifty million EC dollars. The camera panned up to the screen above the heads of the top brass of the RGPF to record the slideshow that was narrated by both the commissioner and Superintendent Telesford.

"Most of the cocaine wasn't staying here, you know," Inspector

Andrews said. "But the good thing is, Grenada holding on to all the money we captured."

"… and in all, eighteen lives were lost this year in the war on White Spice," the commissioner was saying. "This includes six law enforcement personnel."

Andrews picked up a few sorrowful sighs in the room as his team thought about their fallen comrades. It was especially tough to swallow the loss of two Coast Guard sailors when their boat was destroyed during Operation Fish Pot two months ago. He was happy that Big Daddy Johnson and his son, Antonio, had survived the raid. Those two, along with their other family members, faced charges of capital murder for the deaths of the sailors. They were also looking at drug and ammunition-related charges as well as several counts of assault and attempted murder for their roles in firing on law enforcement personnel. CID was also building a case against them for the deadly shooting at Progress Park.

The commissioner continued, "The United States government is so grateful for the sacrifices that we've made that they have donated two new Defender-33 Interceptors to Grenada. We cannot thank the American government enough for their valuable support and assistance in this war on drug trafficking."

"She shoulda ask for a helicopter to assist us with ops," Peters said. "That would give us much better mobility."

"And who go fly it?" Sergeant Charles responded.

"All-you didn't know Inspector could fly helicopter?" Jacob asked no one in particular.

All eyes moved from the TV to Inspector Andrews who was focused on digging into his bowl of soup.

Andrews looked up slowly from his food.

"When I was in South America for three years, I learnt to fly choppers," he confessed. "Don't ask about the missions; they're classified."

Everyone stared at their commanding officer in silence, wondering if they knew who he really was.

"All-you know the Americans will ask us to extradite Big Daddy and Alexander," Andrews said, desperate to change the subject.

A few agents steupsed in annoyance while some rolled their eyes.

"As if dem men didn't commit crimes here too," Jacob remarked indignantly. "Crimes here have less value than those committed against the Americans?"

No one said anything for almost a minute.

"So all the time we focusing on dem Alexanders, was dem Johnson who was more dangerous," Peters broke the silence.

"In a sense it was the Alexanders who put us on to the Johnsons," Andrews noted. "When they crossed paths in Grenville, it changed everything."

"Anybody who could open fire at a police function just to get revenge on somebody have no respect for the law," Sergeant Jacob said.

Several grunts in agreement echoed throughout the room. Some members agreed verbally.

"Correct!"

"You telling me!"

"So what happen to Kellon?" Constable Michaels asked.

"He in hospital still," Peters answered. "He sustained some real serious injuries in that accident."

"But he will be charged with trafficking," Andrews said. "CID trying to pin him to that affair on Levera Beach also."

"You think they have a strong case with that?" Peters asked.

"CID working with us to make a connection," Andrews replied. "The drugs we found in the van the other day come from the same stash as the set we found on Levera Beach in January. Just like the load that American was carrying in April. They all tested positive for the same adulterants."

"Well, that, together with the fact that Shortman was he boy, could help put him away for a long time," Jacob commented.

"I real sorry for he, *oui*," Michaels said. "He alone have to face all dem charges, now that his cousin dead."

"Is the youth we have to feel sorry for," Sergeant Charles said pensively. "The boy lost his brother and his cousin."

"You have a point there," Andrews agreed with the team's psychologist. "I hope he get help."

Sergeant Charles was already thinking of ways to help Jeffrey Alexander. But she was certain that he would never trust the police to help him.

Sergeant Jacob turned to Inspector Andrews.

"So, Inspeck, we do we job so well that we practically wipe out the cocaine business on the island. Wha' we go do now?"

Inspector Andrews chuckled.

"Sarge, you know we job never done," he responded with a wink. "You forget we watching that man in Carriacou?"

The only DS-1 agent originally from Carriacou, Corporal Peters, looked up in surprise.

"Who you talking about now?"

Andrews grinned and said, "Just think about somebody with several boats."

"Inspector, plenty people in Carriacou have boat," Peters said, a bit annoyed that her commanding officer wasn't straight with her.

Inspector Andrews laughed mysteriously and dug into his bowl of soup.

# AUTHOR'S NOTE

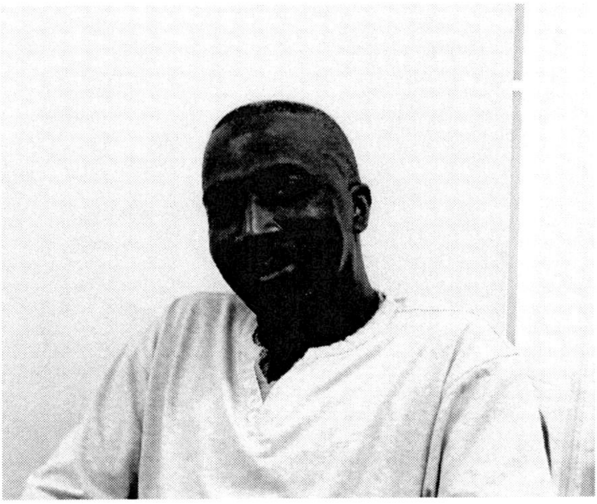

*White Spice* is simply a work of fiction. The book is narrated in British Standard English. Characters communicate often in Grenadian Creole English to reflect the linguistic culture of Grenada. A few terms used by characters point to the influence of French Creole in the Grenadian vernacular.

All the events are figments of my imagination. There is no St. Patrick's Secondary School in Grenada. There is no Coast Guard vessel *Victoria*. There is no DIA. All the events are made up. The Spice Isle is arguably the most peaceful island in the Caribbean .

Research was done mainly to figure out what type of military hardware would be appropriate for specific scenes. To become familiar with police procedures, I interviewed a few officers of several departments of the RGPF. I am grateful to the officers mentioned in the Acknowledgements for providing procedural information that helped me to create a foundation on which to base the story. Thanks also to everyone else who contributed to this project.

CPSIA information can be obtained at www.ICGtesting.com
Printed in the USA
BVOW02s1433121215

430079BV00028BA/394/P

9 781514 355886